Romanesque

OTHER NOVELS BY RALPH McINERNY

Gate of Heaven
The Priest
Rogerson at Bay

Romanesque

Ralph McInerny

HARPER & ROW, PUBLISHERS
New York   Hagerstown
San Francisco   London

FIRST EDITION

Designed by *Janice Stern*

Library of Congress Cataloging in Publication Data

McInerny, Ralph M.
　Romanesque.
　I. Title.
PZ4.M1514Rom　　[PS3563.A31166]　　813′.5′4　　77-6891
ISBN 0-06-012966-2

78　79　80　81　82　10　9　8　7　6　5　4　3　2　1

Kings live in palaces, and pigs in sties,
And youth in expectation. Youth is wise.

—Hilaire Belloc

Romanesque

I

A flock of pilgrims filled the aisle of the plane during much of the transatlantic flight, talking, laughing, drinking, and James Dancey, in the middle seat of three in tourist class, thought them worthy of Chaucer. Of course, the plane was en route to Rome, not Canterbury, but the big, ruddy-faced monsignor who was in charge of the group fostered Dancey's fantasy. He had the look of a preacher of indulgences; he seemed an ecclesiastical con man. Visit the holy places of eternal Rome in the learned company of Monsignor So-and-so. Several times he stopped in the aisle, but Dancey managed to avoid the merry monsignorial eye.

Dancey's image of what a monsignor should be had been formed only recently, by Roberto Nerone, the man from the Vatican he had met at the Italian Embassy in Washington. The raucous airborne shepherd of pilgrims was a far cry from Monsignor Roberto Nerone. But of course the Church casts a wide net. James Dancey smiled. Wide indeed. He still could not believe his good luck and was half numb with the improbability of his destination.

"Do you know him?" the bald man in the window seat asked Dancey.

"The monsignor? No."

"He seems to know you."

The bald man's name was Porres, and his suspicion proved to be contagious. Dancey began to wonder if he truly was an object of special interest to the monsignor. The Church is, after all, an international society.

1

"He seems to know everyone," Dancey said.

"Perhaps."

Porres tugged his blanket up under his chin and closed his eyes. He did not open them again until they had begun the long descent to Rome and breakfast was being served. The stewardess folded the blanket carefully and stowed it overhead.

"Are we on time?" the bald man asked her.

"I'll check."

"Don't bother." An apologetic smile. "We will arrive when we arrive."

"I am anxious to see Rome again," Dancey said. He felt an absurd desire to talk.

"It has changed."

"In what way?"

A little frown and then, again, the apologetic smile. "But everything has changed, has it not? You will love Rome." He might have been reassuring a child with a palpable lie.

"Do you live in Rome?"

Porres nodded and turned to the window. Dancey felt that he had been dismissed.

Fiumicino seemed an armed camp. Porres walked at Dancey's side when they came into customs, as if their seats on the plane had made them permanent companions. The little man seemed gladdened by the sight of *carabinieri,* who, in crushed caps, weapons slung from their shoulders, patrolled the echoing caverns of the terminal building.

When they came into the inspection area, they were directed to a station where no line had yet formed, and Dancey indicated to Porres that he might go first. The little man smiled and gave the suggestion of a bow before placing his attaché case on the table. The inspector drew the case toward him with disdainful eagerness.

Beyond the inspection stations were large glass doors giving onto the main area of the terminal. Here they were still in no man's land. Through those doors lay Italy.

From Italy came two men in black turtleneck sweaters, jostling a customs official aside as they pushed open the door. One of them carried a gun. Dancey watched him drop to one knee, lift the gun and steady his arm with his free hand. He was aiming directly at Porres. Until the man fired, his actions did not even surprise Dancey. But then the gun went off, once, twice, again, and Dancey backed involuntarily away. Porres executed a series of abrupt movements, first crouching, then rising to his toes, finally spinning toward Dancey. The little man's face was contorted with pain, but his eyes swam with a profound, just-acquired wisdom. He took Dancey to the floor with him when he fell.

Dancey struggled free and rolled beneath the inspection table. As he did so, the customs inspector too fell to the floor, blood trickling from his mouth, eyes widened in a blank unseeing stare.

Dancey lay bracketed by Porres and the customs inspector while a small war raged about him. His mind dulled by sleeplessness, unprepared by anything in his past life for this, Dancey squeezed his eyes shut as if by not looking there would be nothing dreadful to see. When he put his hands to his face, his beard felt sticky and warm. He looked at his hands. Blood. The blood of Porres. Dancey did not know this. He was convinced that he himself had been shot. The thought that life was oozing from him, that he was destined to die like Porres and the customs inspector, filled him with terror. And with anger. He began to scream. The louder he screamed, protesting this outrage, the more piercing the sound became. He did not want to die. Not yet. Not ever. The hulk of Porres's body was abhorrent to him. He wanted to lift his foot and push the corpse away, but he sensed that it afforded him protection. He turned, rolling on his side, and found himself looking into the dead eyes of the customs inspector, only inches from his own. While he was being sick, the shooting stopped.

After the bodies of Porres and the customs inspector had been taken away, Dancey realized he was unharmed. Peering out from under the table, he saw the bodies of the two men in black sweaters. He was to learn that eleven people had been killed, but beyond that he could get no coherent account of what had happened or why.

"Ottobre Quindici," a woman inspector said, paging nervously through his passport. "Didn't you hear them shout?"

"What is Ottobre Quindici?"

Her shrug was eloquent. The glass doors beyond had been shattered; there were chips in the marble floor and the concrete pillars. Coverings had been thrown over the places on the floor where men had died. Dancey stared at the spot where Porres had fallen, an X toward which his life had been moving all along. Why?

Several inspection lanes away, the monsignor was lecturing his flock on terrorism. Just so he would instruct them in the catacombs, the Colosseum, the baths of Caracalla. The slaughter, not yet half an hour old, had assumed the status of a historical event.

"The little man's name was Porres," Dancey said.

The inspector looked at him sharply. Did she resent the implication that a passenger was more important than her fallen colleague? She scrawled on a card and handed it to Dancey.

"He said he lived in Rome."

She was not interested. Perhaps knowledge was dangerous. She looked past Dancey at the next person in line.

Dancey picked up his bag and stepped away from the table. He took a last look around, not wanting to lose the fear and horror he had felt. But now there was only movement, bustle, life. Death was always in the wings, ready to swoop out; everyone knew that. The trick was to ignore it. Dancey himself now felt a buoyant joy: he had survived, he was still alive!

He noticed the monsignor talking to an officer of *carabinieri*. The officer turned and looked curiously at Dancey. Was that crazy priest suggesting that Dancey might be of help in the investigation? After all, he had been sitting next to Porres. Dancey headed quickly for the glass doors and, once in the public part of the terminal, did not look back.

"*Signore! Signore!*"

The voice faded away behind him as Dancey moved into the crowd that had gathered when the shooting began.

"James Dancey!"

Surprised, Dancey turned, but it was not the officer of *carabin-*

4

ieri who had called his name. A powerful man in civilian clothes came toward him in a light-footed way.

"I'm in a hurry," Dancey said. "I really can't be of any help to you."

"It is I who am to help you. Ernesto Cielli." He opened a wallet for Dancey's inspection; it seemed a portfolio of credentials, officialdom in miniature. "From the consulate. Have a nice flight?"

Dancey stared at him. "Don't you know what happened? I was nearly killed."

"I know what happened."

"They shot a man named Porres. Ottobre Quindici. They were dressed in black and they burst through the doors...." He babbled on. Cielli nodded, took his arm, led him to a bar, where they sat at a table.

Cielli ordered sweet vermouth. "You'd better have coffee," he advised.

"What the hell is Ottobre Quindici?"

"You must not get a wrong impression of Italy, Dancey. These things happen everywhere now."

"Not to me, they don't."

"Drink your coffee. You are booked at the Columbus Hotel. I will take you there."

"Aren't you going to do something about Porres?"

"He was an American?"

Dancey realized he did not know. "I think so."

"I'll look into it. Wait here."

Dancey watched him go, moving like a halfback through the crowd. He wished he could feel gratitude to Cielli for meeting him; it was irrational to blame the man from the consulate for what had happened. But he could not rid his mind of the image of Porres spinning toward him, his eyes bright with impending eternity. He picked up his cup and drained it.

A familiar voice caused him to turn away. It was that damned monsignor, apparently helping the *carabinieri* find the young American who could be of assistance to them. Dancey wished that Cielli had stayed. There was nothing he could do for Porres now.

5

"He wears a beard. A beard."

Dancey turned. The monsignor was stroking an imaginary beard as he leaned toward the officer. Dancey got to his feet.

"There he is!"

Dancey began to run.

"*Signore! Signore!*"

Dancey headed for a nearby *Uomini*. There were separate doors for entering and leaving the rest room. Dancey went in, hurried across the marble floor, and emerged from the exit. He walked directly into the crowd ringing a newsstand. He did not slacken his pace until he saw a sign indicating public transportation to Rome. Soon he was skipping down a wide staircase, tempted to hysterical laughter at the way he had fooled the man.

But then Dancey remembered Porres and he no longer felt like laughing.

2

Dancey took a bus to the Stazione Termini and from there a cab to
the Columbus Hotel, a converted Renaissance palazzo on the Via
della Conciliazione, just across the Tiber and only a few minutes'
walk from St. Peter's and Vatican City.

The fountain in the courtyard was plashing in the morning sun
when he got out of the cab. Tired as he was, his impulse was to
register, wash, and hit the streets. It had been ten years since he
was in Rome, but ever since the bus entered the city, memories
had been stirring. Some landmarks brought on a strange dizziness,
so vividly did he recall them. It was as if the intervening years had
never been. The Eternal City indeed. And then the cab crossed the
river and there ahead was the huge dome of St. Peter's. Already on
this sunny summer morning the great square teemed with tourists,
carriages, cars, sightseeing buses and ice cream vendors, a whole
excited throng milling about in what seemed the very center of the
world.

The hotel lobby was filled with employees, some in black suits,
some in white shirts and coatless, most in the familiar vests with
green and gold bars, all with a muted meretricious twinkle in their
eye but none daring to move without a nod from one of the
officious-looking men behind the counter.

"Ah, Signor Dancey. *Benvenuto a Roma.*"

Signals were given, a detachment formed at his heels, a large
envelope was produced from safekeeping, his key was given to the
sergeant of the platoon, and Dancey marched with his entourage to

the elevator. He knew he was an officer because he brought up the rear. Only the man who had been given the key entered the elevator with him. The others peeled off to find their way upstairs unaided by the marvels of modern science. Dancey asked the man his name. Giuseppe. He was perhaps forty, of less than middle height, his high-domed head bald, the sides clipped short, thus emphasizing the mustache that made the proportions of his nose acceptable. Like most Italians in hotels and restaurants, he managed to blend an air of disponibility with the faint suggestion that he was an aristocrat fallen on evil times.

"This is not your first time in Rome," he said, and Dancey took it as a compliment to his Italian.

"Nor the last, please God."

Giuseppe liked that. Romanità was bright in his hazel eyes. He promised that everything would be done to make Dancey's stay a pleasant one. The elevator, diffident about defying gravity, finally wheezed to a halt and Dancey followed Giuseppe down the hall. The contingent they had set off with from the desk had re-formed at his door. Giuseppe unlocked it with a flourish and they swarmed inside. Dancey had a handful of five-hundred-lire notes to distribute and a thousand lire for Giuseppe. This had the effect of getting them out of the room quickly. Giuseppe bowed out last, his smile a pianoforte of gratitude.

The now-opened balcony doors gave Dancey a view of the courtyard with its fountain and he went outside to savor the scene. He had forgotten how Rome reveals herself in vedute, as if no matter where one looked, a paintable prospect offered itself. Or more likely a photographable one.

A redhead in a long green robe stook on the next balcony and she smiled across at him. "Roma," she cried theatrically, extending her arms. With her shoulders thrown back, her breasts blossomed like bombs.

"Roma," Dancey agreed. "Il sole è caldo, vero?"

As if surprised by her own forwardness, the redhead dropped her eyes. "Sì, signore." She lisped. Dancey found this charming. But the redhead darted inside.

Dancey too went inside. He sat on the bed. He meant to see what was in the envelope he had been given at the desk, but it was a mistake to sit down, particularly on the bed. Fatigue overwhelmed him. He fell back, dropping the envelope on the floor, stared at the scrollwork on the ceiling, closed his eyes. Against his lids, like a film rewinding, his trip, the past few weeks, spun past—Porres, Washington, Roberto Nerone, and then he was asleep.

He had received his third degree in May, sitting on the mall with nearly a thousand others, most of them there for a B.A. or B.S. Some years before, he himself had been dubbed a bachelor and that, thank God, in one sense, he remained. Subsequently he earned his master's. Master of arcane lore, jack of no trade. In May, along with seventy-seven others, he had been publicly recognized as a doctor of philosophy.

The commencement speaker was an overweight black from one of the Washington bureaus, who lectured his audience on the injustices that had been done his race. His speech was half a dozen years out of sync. He was gainfully employed. The whites he addressed were destined for menial jobs at best, the unemployment office at worst, perhaps a life of crime. Dancey felt a criminal growl gather in his throat, the growl of the oppressed. No academic job awaited him. He had been overcome. The hooding ceremony was like a requiem, the doctoral colors descending on him like an albatross. He had reached the pinnacle of academic achievement. He had seen the future and it did not work. And neither, it seemed, would he. At least not in the profession for which he had been trained.

He had written two hundred letters of application; he had haunted the flesh markets of professional meetings. Praline, his dissertation director, had lied on his behalf in an unctuous letter which, along with several more realistic recommendations, lay in his dossier in the university placement bureau. That dossier had been requested only twice, once by mistake. A research fellowship, applied for without hope, had not been awarded, although he was named an alternate. If someone died or lost interest in a free ride,

Dancey would step in. Fat chance.

His area was medieval studies with an emphasis on theology. His dissertation dealt with the quodlibetal questions of an anonymous Parisian master of the thirteenth century. He was overspecialized, exotic, developed in all the wrong directions to survive the current depression in the academic marketplace. It seemed inescapable that he had, from a practical point of view, wasted six years of his life.

The greatest irony of all was that he had known this beyond a shadow of a doubt during his years of graduate work. He had watched others finish before him, people of whose talent there was no question, who yet failed to find academic employment. He knew his prospects were dim, knew it but did not believe it. One does not regard oneself as merely an instance of a type. He was himself alone, James Thomas Dancey, B.A., M.A., Ph.D. cum laude.

After the ceremony, he skulked out of town without saying goodbye to Praline—an unemployed Ph.D. felt the need of a leper's bell when confronting the tenured faculty—and went on impulse to Minneapolis, where he took a room on the third floor of a huge house near Lake Calhoun. Once it must have sheltered some impossibly affluent family. Now it was carved up into what the absent owner playfully called apartments. One-room apartments. The house had stucco walls covered with ivy, a tile roof, and was surrounded by great old oaks: it looked cool and was not. At a discount house, Dancey bought a huge floor fan whose roar suggested that a medium-sized plane was warming up in his doorway. The woman he reported to at the unemployment office thought he was a condescending bastard, but then he thought she was an officious bitch. You would have thought she was dispensing money from her private funds.

"Is there any other kind of work you are prepared to do?" Her eyes were pressed shut while she spoke and, the words uttered, her lips became again a not quite healed wound.

"I devoted six years of my life preparing myself to teach medieval thought," he said plaintively.

"There are no jobs for teachers of medieval thought."

"That is one of the things I learned."

"Have you tried professional placement bureaus?"

His sardonic smile had a wider target than this poor overworked wench. Doubtless she had an unsatisfactory husband, children who had not turned out well, a boss she could not stand. He thought without snobbery, though of course he was a snob, that he was not a typical client. Her initial reaction to all the information he had crowded into the modest space the form provided for educational experience told him that. He was almost ashamed of his attainments. We grow dumber by degrees.

His mother provided whatever thin excuse there was for going to Minneapolis. She had remarried twice since his father's death and her new husband was a Minneapolitan. He was several years younger than his bride, had two children still in school; Dancey wondered if the whole thing was not a desperate effort on his mother's part to recapture her youth and the stability her life had had when his father was still alive. If living in various foreign countries as the representative of a major American oil company qualifies as stability.

"You can stay with us," she said dubiously when he told her he might remain in Minneapolis.

"No."

She seemed relieved. "Bill will insist on it."

"I've rented a room. An apartment."

"Minneapolis is a lovely city. What will you do?"

"I'm on welfare."

He could almost believe that it had been for the purpose of eliciting her shocked reaction that he had applied for unemployment.

"Didn't you finish school?"

"Oh yes."

"You got your doctorate?"

He nodded.

"But surely you can get a teaching job with your degree?"

He tried to explain to her what had happened in the groves of academe. There had been an overproduction of people with advanced degrees, the glut subsidized by the government. No one had taken sufficiently into account the demographics of future college-age kids. It was not so much that the curve was down as that it was no longer rising. Meanwhile, as expansion of faculty stopped, those in place achieved tenure and there were no more places. Or as bad as no more places. The few there were tended to go to blacks and women because of something called affirmative action. Thanks to Yankee slave traders, Southern planters and the division of the sexes, he languished unemployed in Minneapolis.

"You are not going to be on welfare."

His mother was wearing a tennis costume and her hair was streaked from the sun. Her complexion, if slightly leathery and weatherworn, was taut. He wished that she would take off her sunglasses, but then she probably wished that he would take off his. Behind her, on the clay courts, her stepchildren were smashing tennis balls about. Beyond them was the clubhouse, the pool and ultimately, the golf course.

"I'll speak to Bill," she said.

"Don't."

In the end, ten days later, he accepted her offer to finance his return to Washington, where they understood unemployment. He told her it would be well for him to be near his university. Just in case. How eager she was to believe the wisdom of this.

Bill came along when his mother brought the ticket and drove Dancey to the airport. Bill stayed in the car, but his mother insisted on coming into the terminal. Bill's farewell wave was expansive and relieved. A twenty-six-year-old son did not jibe with his new wife's image as a young matron. There were five twenties in the ticket wallet.

"Thanks for the money," he said, after he had checked his luggage. He was carrying a briefcase and wearing a suit and tie. He felt like someone he used to know. "I'll pay Bill back."

"The money is from me," she said a little sharply.

"I'll keep in touch."

"Good."

12

It was an awkward moment, in which they were reminded that she had borne him. She took off her sunglasses now. There were little wrinkles at the edges of her eyes. More surprisingly, there were tears in them. He embraced her with his free arm and kissed her cheek. She moved and pressed her lips to his. She said into his shoulder, "We never did have a decent talk."

About his father? About the way it used to be? That was a talk they were unlikely ever to have. It was then that, almost with surprise, he realized he had resented his mother's being alive and with a new family when his father was dead. He kissed her again, stepped back, smiled in his most independent manner and said good-bye. He was trying to let her know that everything was fine, nothing was her fault, he did not blame her.

Twenty yards down the ramp, after he had gone through security, he looked back to see her still standing there. She waved. It was like a blessing. They had had their decent talk after all.

During the week following his return to Washington, Dancey had been seldom sober. That had been the nadir. When he came out of it, he telephoned Praline, intending to wallow in self-pity and treat his director as an accessory to the crime. Incredibly, Praline had good news. Had not Dancey heard? The research fellowship had come through after all. James Dancey would be financed out of the taxpayer's pocket to further pursue his studies at the Vatican Library. This was confirmed by a call to the State Department. He was invited to a reception at the Italian Embassy.

The reception line at the Italian Embassy on Fuller Street consisted of signora, the ambassador, the apostolic delegate to the United States, and Cardinal Manuccio of the Vatican Library. A white girl with a pink afro preceded Dancey in the line and he was glad to have her run interference for him. He suspected she was a crasher. Over the years, he himself had often fattened uninvited on Embassy Row, something surprisingly easy to do. Signora had a long lined face, a large well-shaped nose, and great sad eyes set in purplish bags. Dancey was conscious of knuckles and rings when he took her hand.

"Buon giorno, signora. Mi chiamo Dottore Dancey."

"Lei parla Italiano con una buona pronuncia, dottore." She passed him on to her husband. *"Il signore parla Italiano perfettamente."*

"Ha passato del tempo in Italia?" the ambassador asked.

"Si. Dieci anni fa. In Roma. Con la mia famiglia."

The ambassador conveyed this trivia to the delegate, though not in Italian. The bearded American had lived with his family in Rome ten years ago. The delegate was Belgian, a youngish-looking man, tall, bald, warily diplomatic. He put it back into Italian for Cardinal Manuccio. The cardinal was a squat square figure of a man in a scarlet cassock, whose pudgy hands played with a bejeweled pectoral cross. Dancey had the feeling that the cardinal would have preferred blessing him to shaking his hand. The prelate's smile squeezed his eyes half shut and he seemed to be studying Dancey. Would he recognize the name? He did not.

"Dottore," was all the cardinal said before turning his princely gaze to the next person in line.

"Well, you made a hit," the pink afro said. "What were you telling them?"

"That the woman ahead of me was armed and dangerous, but if we all kept our heads she could be subdued."

"Only by food and drink. Come on."

Scotch and soda, wines, canapés galore, an elegant room filled with beautiful people, the pink afro at his elbow, Dancey found it hard to believe that he had been so recently on the brink of despair.

"You drink Scotch and soda in the Italian Embassy?"

The speaker was a tall cleric Dancey had noticed in the background of the reception line, lounging against a wall. The priest bowed when they turned to him, first to the girl, then to Dancey. It seemed a little rite. One half expected incense to rise.

"I am Roberto Nerone. The companion of his eminence the cardinal." To Dancey he said, "You speak Italian well."

"Not as well as you speak English."

Nerone accepted the compliment with a nod. He held a glass of sherry in long pale fingers. Dark wavy hair, almond eyes, an otherworldly expression. His smile was utterly impersonal, particularly when it was turned on the girl.

"And what does a cardinal's companion do?" she asked saucily.

"Smooth his path. Make straight his ways." A quick smile. "I congratulate you on your fellowship, Dr. Dancey. Could you have dinner with me tonight?"

Perhaps daunted by this indication that Dancey was not an interloper, the girl drifted away. Dancey watched her go as if she represented his freeloading youth. Nerone's remark was a reminder that his life had taken on point and purpose.

They ate at the Café di Napoli, a few blocks from the old State Department building, and Dancey found that he was not at all uncomfortable to be sitting in a restaurant with a priest.

"You are not a Catholic, Dr. Dancey?"

"No."

"Yet you pursued your studies at Georgetown?"

"That's right." Being a student at Georgetown had not involved him much with the Catholic Church. He had been aware of it as an ambience, but it was at some distance from the daily doings of graduate students. He did not tell Nerone that Georgetown had reawakened the fascination with Catholicism he had felt as a boy in Rome and that had made his parents uneasy. Then it had been a matter of pageantry, religion as ritual, Renaissance churches and opulent splendor. When he was a graduate student, the attraction was on another level. He had conceived a profound interest in Thomas Aquinas. This had happened at a time when Aquinas's stock had declined to almost zero among Catholics, though once he had been the only company listed. Dancey had found an old Jesuit to guide him through the *Summa theologiae*.

"I did become a Thomist," he told Nerone.

"A Thomist!" Nerone's smile revealed a set of perfect teeth. "What a rarity you are. Tell me about your fellowship."

Dancey was delighted to. The stipend was modest, but it was meant to support him for the equivalent of a semester. His transportation would be provided. Dancey felt enormously grateful, but it was difficult to form an image of his benefactor. If the grant had come from a private foundation, he could thank the grudging heirs of some repentant robber baron, but the United States Government in the form of the National Endowment for the Humanities was an abstract entity. When he had applied for the grant, Praline advised him to think of it as buying a ticket in the lottery. Whom does the holder of the lucky ticket thank?

The girl he had spoken to at the State Department seemed as good a target as any for his gratitude.

"The consulate will transfer money to your account," she had told Dancey. "Other than that, you're on your own." She sounded wistful. "Been to Rome before?"

"Yes."

"I envy you."

Dispensing largess was only her job. Like a teller in a bank, she was rich with other people's money. Dancey felt obliged to tell her where he would have been if this grant had not come through.

"This is a great opportunity for me," Dancey said to Nerone in the Café di Napoli.

"We shall be pleased to welcome you to the Vatican Library."

Nerone. Nerone. The name was familiar, he did not know why. A silent smile seemed the safest course. He should have suspected Nerone would be connected with the library. Why else would he have known of Dancey's fellowship?

Nerone said, "You know that our manuscript collection is on microfilm at St. Louis University?"

"I spent a month there because of it. And another at Notre Dame, where the Ambrosian Library is on microfilm."

"That was done as a convenience to scholars like yourself. Not that microfilm can substitute for the manuscript itself." Nerone leaned forward. "It was also done as a precaution."

How often through the centuries priceless remnants of the past have been wiped out by war and natural disaster. Nerone reminded Dancey of the Florence flood, when the Arno spilled over its banks to threaten Renaissance treasures and actually to damage many.

"The critical edition of Ockham's commentary on Peter Lombard was nearly washed away," Dancey said.

"Even valuable things might have been lost."

Nerone invited Dancey to think too of the fanatic who had attacked Michelangelo's *Pietà* in St. Peter's itself. Given the present political situation in Italy, the Vatican was painfully aware that the cultural treasures entrusted to it were vulnerable as perhaps never before.

Another sack of Rome? Perhaps. Nerone did not seem to find it far-fetched to see the current situation on an analogy with the barbarian invasions. Terror has become a commonplace of modern life. And, he added significantly, if the original Vatican Library is in jeopardy, the same must be said of its replica in St. Louis.

"We cannot underestimate the fanaticism of these new iconoclasts, Dr. Dancey."

It was an odd conversation to be having in the crowded, happy little restaurant in Washington, but Dancey found Nerone's point as plausible as his tone of voice. There were cultural Luddites around, no doubt about that. Attacks on computer centers were only symptomatic. Paintings had been slashed and statues mutilated in America too. Even if these were the deeds of isolated fanatics, the results were nonetheless irreparable. And Dancey had the growing sense that Nerone had introduced this topic for some reason other than to lament the times.

"Does this have something to do with my fellowship?"

Nerone's expression was pained. "This is very difficult, Dr. Dancey. In order to confide in you, I need your agreement to help, and you can scarcely agree to help unless I confide in you."

"But it has to do with the safety of the Vatican Library?"

"Would that be sufficient motive for you?"

"Is this why I was granted the fellowship?"

Nerone did not hesitate. "It will not be withdrawn if you refuse. You need have no fear of that. It was a great courtesy on the part of your government to permit me to see the list of applicants and to make a recommendation."

For a moment, Dancey had felt deflated, but Nerone's words now filled him with an almost intolerable delight. "Why me?" he asked, and was himself surprised by his seemingly casual tone.

"Because you have the academic credentials, because you speak Italian. Do you think your friends might be surprised that you have been awarded the fellowship?"

A graduate student does not have friends. He has competitors. Even so, Dancey felt no impulse to bruit his good fortune about. Let Praline spread the word if he wanted to, perhaps suggesting that those who wrote dissertations with him were taken care of one way or another. That the fellowship might be compromised by any hesitation on his part, no matter what Nerone had said, decided him.

"Of course I'll help. What do you want me to do?"

"Good. I speak now in deepest confidence, Dancey." Nerone paused. "We intend to put the entire Vatican Library manuscript collection on microfiche, in secrecy, as further insurance against what the future might bring."

"Why in secrecy?" Dancey's voice dropped. He felt that he was being initiated into a project of immense significance. His slight frown was meant to discourage the smile that would have loved to curl the corners of his mouth. The Vatican Library had chosen James Dancey!

"For several reasons. First, this is being done solely as a precaution, not as a convenience to scholars. For it to become known would make it the target of the kind of people we fear. It would be more difficult to maintain secrecy if we worked from the St. Louis University copies, and of course those microfilms were made some time ago, when the technique was not as advanced at it became. Today there are more efficient and satisfactory methods. Microfiche. Second ... " Nerone took a sip of wine, but his eyes did not leave Dancey. "Second, there is opposition within the Vatican itself. Indeed, the opponents of the project have been allowed to think they have prevailed. We are to proceed sub rosa."

18

"Won't it be terribly expensive?"

"It will. Cardinal Manuccio has been having confidential discussions with government officials here. Fortunately, the importance of the project is recognized. Funds will be forthcoming, on condition that the microfiched library is stored in the United States. This seems a reasonable demand. Are you interested?"

Of course he was interested. Like a lover on the rebound, he was interested. His career had been all but checkmated, he had wallowed for a week in drunken despair, and now he had received a fellowship and was being recruited by the most esteemed research library in the world. He had no idea how helping Nerone would fit in with his personal research, but there could be no opposition between the two projects. In the Dark Ages, monks had cherished classical works in their monasteries, painstakingly copying them in scriptoria, diffusing them throughout Europe. Hardly more than a trickle, of course, but much of our knowledge of Greek and Latin authors depends on their efforts. In the Renaissance, the most eminent figures contributed wealth and time to the recovery of the achievements of the past. In order for the past to be discovered, it must exist. The thought of playing some part in the preservation of the contents of the Vatican Library excited him. Who would have refused conscription in the bucket brigade when the library at Alexandria was burning? Not James Dancey. He assured Nerone that he was interested.

"I was certain you would be. When do you leave for Rome?"

"As soon as my passport is ready."

He told Nerone what he had been told. Someone from the consulate would meet him.

"I shall be booked into the Columbus Hotel."

"Excellent."

"Monsignor Nerone, you realize how flattered I am."

"You are perfect for our purposes, Dr. Dancey." Nerone finished his wine and wiped his lips. "I shall contact you in Rome, then. At the Columbus Hotel."

3

A ringing descended into the dark like a dentist's drill probing for a yet more sensitive nerve. Dancey came awake and was relieved to find that it was only the telephone.

"Roberto Nerone here. You have arrived."

"Yes. Yes. I fell asleep." He looked at his watch and then at the window. He had not been asleep an hour.

"May I come to your room?"

"Are you in the hotel?"

He was. Dancey asked Nerone to give him a minute before coming up. It had been a mistake not to wash before taking a nap. His eyes were red, the snarl of his beard unsightly. His clothes looked as if he had slept in them after rolling around on the floor, and no wonder. The image of Porres flickered in his mind. He wished he had asked Nerone to give him ten minutes. There was a tap at the door—some minute—and Dancey went to answer it.

Nerone was even more impressive in his long robe than he had been in street clothes. There was red piping on his cassock and the buttons too were red.

"Monsignore," Dancey said. "Come in."

"I see you were not injured at the airport."

"The man who sat beside me was killed." Immediately he regretted having said it. Putting Porres's death into words domesticated it, tamed it, reduced it to chitchat. "I'm surprised you know of the airport incident already."

Nerone made a gesture. "In any case, you are here, safe and sound. And very tired?"

"I'm all right."

Nerone was making an inspection of the room. "An interesting building," he said. "And it is convenient to the Vatican. Were you given a package at the desk?" But he had already seen the envelope lying beside the bed.

"From Cardinal Manuccio. I haven't had time to open it."

"Would you do so now?"

Inside were half a dozen passes and several letters embossed with important-looking seals bearing the title of the pontifical commission of which Cardinal Manuccio was head. Dancey was described in elaborate prose as a young American scholar currently in Italy on a grant from his government in order to pursue research. His eminence would be grateful for any consideration shown Dr. Dancey, etc., etc. Dancey's photograph, the same as on his passport—they had asked for half a dozen at the State Department—was affixed to the card that was his entrée to the Biblioteca Apostolica Vaticana. It was made out to Sig. Prof. James Dancey and was valid until December 15. On the back of the card was a legend enumerating the obligations he took on as a user of the library. Among other things, he obliged himself not to ask for codices from reserve without first having made a written request to the prefect in which he made clear his expertise and the absolute need to see them, *"persuaso che tali cimeli devono essere trasmessi incolumi alla posterità."* This printed conviction that the library's treasures should be passed on unharmed to posterity echoed Nerone's remarks in Washington. Dancey suggested it could serve as the motto of the microfiching project.

"Exactly."

"It is groups like Ottobre Quindici you had in mind, wasn't it?"

Nerone was startled. "How do you mean?"

"That is what the airport terrorists called themselves. Ottobre Quindici."

"I see." After a moment he said, "You must present your papers when you appear at the library."

"To the prefect?"

A deprecating smile. "The prefect of the Apostolic Vatican Library is Roberto Nerone."

And so he was. It said so in the papers and documents Dancey held. Nerone seemed young for so eminent a position.

"Now then, Dr. Dancey. Have you been contacted by your consulate?"

Dancey laughed and told Nerone of the encounter with Cielli at the airport. It seemed less a joke as he proceeded. Nerone was frowning.

"I am the first one to contact you here at the hotel?"

"Yes."

Nerone thought about that. "Very well. We shall have lunch nearby. I shall call the desk and tell them where you can be reached." He picked up the phone. "No doubt you will want to wash."

Dancey felt a bit like a child being sent to clean up before a meal. His rancor was not deep. After all, he was in Rome.

Nerone broke bread with long, fastidious fingers while they awaited their cannelloni. His manner had not warmed appreciably and Dancey began to feel that he was being treated as an underling. That is what he was, of course, but resentment grew in him, aided by the weariness that had returned in the sunny street. He felt that Nerone had shown inadequate concern about the danger he had faced at the airport.

"These things happen everywhere, Dancey. You are safer here than in America."

Dancey was not sure he liked that slur. Oh, the hell with it. If Nerone wanted to be businesslike, it was all right with him.

"Tell me exactly what I am to do."

"What you are told." Nerone's smile was lukewarm. "I mean that there must be no improvising. The modus operandi of the library is centuries old and the less that is done to disturb the sensibilities of the staff, the better."

22

"You said there has been disagreement about the project. How many know of it?"

"The number is not important. The man in charge of the project is Ulrich Strommer."

"Do I report to him?"

"You will meet him, that is routine. Dancey, our arrangement is our arrangement, do you understand? We shall proceed in such a way that the right hand will not know what the left is doing."

"Why?"

"I told you that we are doing this as a precautionary measure. It must be swaddled in secrecy. It must be done as if it were not being done at all. That is why it cannot be done in the library itself."

"Surely you don't mean the manuscripts will be removed from the library."

"That is exactly what I mean. For this we need an outsider. You."

"But how . . . "

Their cannelloni arrived and it would have been sacrilegious not to give it their undivided attention. Nerone, having sampled it, rolled his eyes for the benefit of the waiter. Dancey added his own congratulations, but it was Nerone's praise that was wanted.

The restaurant was on a side street, about a block from the hotel. Nerone had taken a table inside, but there were others on the sidewalk. Dancey, facing the street, was able to enjoy the passing parade along with his meal. He would have enjoyed both more if he were not confused as to how exactly he was supposed to aid in the microfiching project.

"How long will it take?"

"I don't know."

"You must have a rough idea."

"I prefer to speak only when I can be precise."

"But I don't understand what you want me to do."

"Of course you don't. For now, you will acquaint yourself with the library. Get to know Strommer. My instructions will make sense after you know the library well."

"But you want me to take manuscripts out of the library?"

Nerone looked at him a full minute and then nodded slowly. "Yes. You will act alone but you will not be alone. Remember why we are doing this. That is the important thing. There are those who feel we have already taken sufficient insurance against disaster, with the St. Louis microfilming. Some of us disagree. Recent political events confirm our apprehensions."

"Ottobre Quindici?"

Nerone frowned. "I was thinking of the elections. But let us drop the subject for now. *Va bene?* Good. Wine?"

Why not? It had been a long flight and he was eager to taste the delights of Rome. He was confirmed in this thought by the sight of a young woman in a floral dress who had taken one of the sidewalk tables. Nerone now seemed as anxious to get lunch over with as he was, but an Italian's idea of a quick meal is not yours or mine. The wine, a delightful white, was balm of a sort. It was Nerone's treat, and after he paid the waiter, he went in search of the proprietor to offer his congratulations in person. Dancey took it into his head that he was in the company of Duncan Hines. Remember Duncan Hines? Signora bobbed in from the back and Dancey was introduced. Their name was Posti and they were clearly impressed by Nerone, even commenting on the fine cut of his clerical garments. Dancey announced that he would like to toast the Postis. The wine on top of jet lag had gotten to him. Nerone failed to grasp the keen wit of the remark. But then he seemed never to have heard of Duncan Hines either.

"They knew me before I was a priest," Nerone said with a smile when they were outside. "They are good people. You will want to learn if the consulate has been trying to reach you."

"I may phone them."

"Good. And then you can play the tourist a bit. Did you bring a camera?" Nerone's smile was ironic.

Dancey watched him walk away, for all the world as if he were sweeping up the aisle of a church. People stepped aside, opening a way for him, as deferential as the Postis. Dancey was sure Nerone would rise high in the Church and, with the great dome of St. Peter's as background, he thought of how high high could be in Rome. It was a nice thought that he had just had cannelloni with a man who might one day be thought *papabile*.

4

"James Dancey?"

The girl in the floral dress frowned up at him from the sidewalk table.

"Don't you remember me?"

"No." The admission would have been impossible to make, given a moment's thought. He would far prefer to be flooded with tender memories of this girl. Her black hair was cut short, forming a nimbus about her full, softly molded face, whose large eyes now held a scolding expression. She made Dancey feel like an impostor. After all, she knew his name.

"Mr. Durham," she said.

"English and tennis coach."

"Miss Heenan."

"Hyena Heenan." He sat down at her table.

"Count Dracula."

"Mr. Krebs."

She laughed. "See? You are the Jim Dancey who attended the international school here in Rome."

"And so did you, obviously. What's your name?"

Her smile gave way to a pout. "You really don't know?"

"I'm sorry."

"I'm kidding. Why should you remember? I was several classes below you."

"Even so."

"Didn't you live in Vigna Clara?"

"Parioli. What is your name?"

"Polly. Polly Bertello. What are you doing in Rome?"

"Have you lived here since school?"

"Good Lord, no. I've been back a lot, though. My uncle has an apartment and I could always stay with him." For some ten minutes, with indifferent results, they tried to reconstruct the past. "What do you do?" she asked.

"Research. Study." It sounded even remoter than it was. "I'm here to do some things in the Vatican Library."

The waiter came with her coffee. She loaded it with sugar and stirred the foaming mixture vigorously. "Married?"

"No. Are you?"

"Not anymore."

"What happened?"

Her eyes took on a bewildered look. It made no sense, but seated there at that diminutive sidewalk table with the warm Roman sunlight slanting down, he felt suddenly close to this girl he could not for the life of him remember. He tried to think of her as an old friend with whom he had just been reunited. They had attended the same school. He could not remember her, but how many of his old classmates did he remember now? Perhaps it was the mixture of a shared past and being strangers that made it easy for her to talk.

"I don't know. Isn't that crazy? You'd think you'd know what went wrong when a marriage falls apart, but I don't. I haven't a clue. It just wasn't there suddenly. And then he wasn't there either. And here I am." Her smile was a bleak attempt.

"And here you are." He was sorry he had asked. He was almost sorry he had sat down. Someone this quick to tell her troubles seemed almost happy to have them. With a sunny free afternoon before him, Dancey had no intention of getting tied down to a neurotic divorcee.

"How long will you be in Rome, Jim?"

"That's not clear yet."

"What sort of research do you do?"

"It would bore you."

"Try me."

"I'd love to." It just came out and when it had he was sure it shouldn't have, but a moment later he didn't know. She made a little face, but she really did not seem displeased. He thought it best to let the racket of the traffic assert itself for a time.

She said, "Do you get back here often?"

"This is my first visit in ten years."

"It's changed," she said, and he remembered Porres on the plane.

"So have I."

He thought of the kid he had been. He thought of the school, of their apartment. He thought of his father. It was as though his memories of his father sharpened here and he wondered what it would be like to see that building in Parioli where they had all been so happy, his father and mother and himself.

"What is it?" Polly asked.

"I was thinking of where we lived."

"Want to go look?"

"Do you mean it?"

She drank off her coffee, opened her purse and put some money on the table. "You said Parioli? That's not far. My car is around the corner."

But she headed straight for the street and started across, weaving through traffic as if she had had a private revelation that she would live to be a hundred. Or perhaps she was suicidal. More likely she was relying on the Italian driver's inability to ignore the sight of a pretty girl crossing the street. Deference to her, even to the point of actually slowing down to avoid hitting her, was not a loss of machismo, but an instance of it. His own passage, a step or two behind, was more precarious. He actually touched cars with his fingertips as they sped past. He had difficulty concealing how terrified he had been when he joined her on the opposite side of the street. To have survived the airport massacre only to be nailed by a Fiat would have been cruel.

"You're really going to do research at the Vatican?"

"Didn't you believe me before?"

"Why should I? You didn't even remember who I was."

This was a logic he did not attempt to follow. It was difficult enough to keep up with her on the crowded sidewalk. And then they turned a corner and become involved in grand opera.

Polly's car, a dark-blue sports model, had been parked in such a way that it blocked the entrance of a garage. A car, backed halfway out of the garage, in turn blocked the sidewalk. Frustrated pedestrians were shouting at the driver to get his godforsaken car off the sidewalk. He stood beside it, addressing the heavens, calling down curses on whoever had left that mother-defiling Fiat in his driveway. A kid had jumped onto the bumper of the sports car and now began to bounce it. He was joined by others. Polly, taking this as cue, entered the fray. Her Italian was impassioned and eloquent; it took flight from the obvious fact that she was in the wrong. She demanded to be shown the sign forbidding her to park where she was. The driver of the other car, smiling malevolently, obliged her. His wrath seemed diluted by lust as his eyes traveled over Polly's body. The kids on her back bumper began to make explicit comments on her breasts. She turned on them in fury, her eyes sparking, and unleashed what Dancey took to be an answering stream of obscenities. The kids jumped down, grinning in admiration.

"Polly," Dancey said. "Polly, take it easy."

She turned and told him calmly to get into the car. "I'm not through with this guy."

She strode up to the blocked driver and swung her purse. He grabbed for it, caught it, tugged. A fatal mistake. The onlookers, who had drawn in a closer ring around the drama, howled at his want of gallantry. Cries of "Thief" went up. The kid who had first jumped onto Polly's bumper began to shout for a policeman. The driver pressed Polly's purse into her hands. When she had it, she took another swing at him. Cheers. The man lifted his arms to defend himself and Polly slammed her purse against his raised forearms, turned on her heel and marched to her car. Cheers. Applause.

Her face was flushed with satisfaction when she slipped in beside Dancey. The sight of the cowed driver, who had after all been in the right, prevented Dancey from congratulating her. But Polly seemed to have forgotten the episode already. She started the car, gunned the motor several times, and took off with a spinning of wheels. The car tipped dramatically as she took the corner.

Her driving matched her performance in the street. She was reckless, inspired and lucky, Dancey, trying to relax, gripped a dashboard handle and braced his feet. The one thing that could be said for Polly's driving was that she concentrated on it. Indeed, her chin thrust forward, there was a glint in her eyes and a tight little smile on her lips.

"My God," Dancey cried when a car entering from a side street nosed to a stop inches from his door. Polly had neither let up on the gas nor given any sign that she had seen the car coming.

"Basically, Roman traffic is a huge game of chicken," she explained. "Did you ever drive here?"

"Does anyone? They're all kamikazes."

"You get used to it."

Dancey doubted that very much.

A block of buildings, one different from the others, not so much in appearance as in the memories it evoked. A strangely familiar entrance. A neighborhood of strangers. Sitting beside Polly, surveying the street that had once captured all the overtones of the word "home" for him, Dancey found that he had no desire to see a face that would connect him with his past in this place. But that was as little likely as that his dead father should emerge from the building and climb into his car.

"Want to go inside?" Polly asked.

"No."

"Disappointed?"

"No. Maybe. I don't know."

"Let's go see my uncle! His apartment isn't far from here."

Dancey looked at her. She had the wholesome smile of a 4-H girl suggesting he drink more milk. "Is that where you're staying?"

"No." She put the car in gear and pulled away from the curb.

Did she have other plans, the uncle a ruse? Dancey felt a kind of panic. His brains seemed loose in his head, turning like a gyroscope, seeking equilibrium, fighting off the effects of a long flight, a short night, an airport massacre followed by a flood of memories, not to mention the harrowing drive with Polly. It would be just his luck to encounter an amorous female in his present weakened condition. Not that he was plagued by such encounters when sound of wind and limb, but he liked to think of himself as ready, on red alert, at all times. The pert, pixielike Polly with her dairy-maid smile, daunting profanity and heedless driving was everything those dirty-mouthed kids had said she was.

"Polly, I'd like to meet your uncle, but . . . "

"Of course you would. Your father worked for him."

"He did!"

"International Oil. How do you think I remembered you?"

"Don't ask me."

"You were the upperclassman, Mr. Dancey's son Jim, why didn't I just introduce myself?" She glanced at him. "I had a terrible time at school, at first. Bad marks, no friends, interested in nothing and no one."

"Does your uncle still work for Intoil?"

She laughed. "He says he's retired."

Polly had turned into a narrow street. She swung sharply into a driveway and brought the hood of the car up to a gate. She touched the horn; a moment later the gate opened and she drove in. They dropped down an inclined drive covered by a latticed roof supporting grapevines. Dancey had a brief glimpse of sun slanting through leaves and lattice. The drive angled around the building. One of the garage doors was open and Polly, backing and filling, maneuvered inside. The garage door was closing behind them before she turned off the motor.

Dancey's legs were rubbery with fatigue as they crossed the garage to an elevator. What in hell was he doing running around Rome with this girl? He should be at his hotel, in bed, trying to get his body synchronized with the public time of Rome. But the sight of Polly punching the elevator button and turning to face him stilled such churlish thoughts. Her uncle would not be home. He himself could be revivified by a stiff drink or, if necessary, a cold shower. Another drink, the two of them side by side on the settee, recalling old times, lamenting the fleet finger with which time traced their lives, turning to one another for consolation . . .

They emerged into a spacious hall furnished in such a way that it could not possibly be a common foyer. An Oriental rug was cast over the marble floor, and somehow cast was the word: there was something splendidly careless about laying that carpet at the entrance of an elevator. On the wall directly before him was a framed medieval parchment, Gregorian chant, the *Quotiescumque* syllabically riding the diamond-shaped neums. The illumination of the initial Q, while faded, seemed, in the foyer, still brilliant, and Dancey suspected that the lighting had been devised to produce just this effect. An artful modern illumination of a medieval illuminated manuscript.

There were three closed doors, one of which now opened to reveal a dwarflike woman in maid's costume, her outthrust chin sporting various growths. She fixed a cold eye on Dancey and cleared her throat in welcome to Polly.

"Is my uncle in?"

The uncle, said Caterina, for this was the maid's name, was taking a nap, but she would wake signore. For all her gruff manner, the little woman was obviously glad to see Polly.

The room they were admitted to was dark and Polly tugged at the drapes. Sunlight spilled into a room that Dancey thought belonged in the Doria-Pamphili palazzo on the Corso rather than in this modern building on Mount Parioli. He would have been more impressed if he had been less tired. He took in the room the way the jaded tourist sees his thirty-sixth sumptuous salon as he is hustled through Versailles. The most important item of furniture

33

was the chair beside him. He collapsed into it. Polly went after the maid, and he could hear her voice, a lilting reveille, a little girl's voice. Dancey closed his eyes and massaged his lids. To die, to sleep . . .

Before sleep could come he heard a new voice. Shaking his head, opening and shutting his eyes swiftly several times, Dancey heaved to his feet as a tall, white-haired, undeniably American figure strode into the room.

"James Dancey?" he said warmly, enclosing his visitor's hand. "This is indeed a delight. I thought Polly was pulling an old man's leg. I knew your daddy. I knew your mother. And"—his smile became avuncular—"I knew you when you were no higher than the hind leg of a pissant."

"A pissant!" Polly squealed. "What on earth is a pissant?"

"I am Nathaniel Gainer. It's too much to expect that my niece would introduce us."

Dancey nodded stupidly. The hinges of his jaw threatened to creak open in a yawn in the midst of all this joviality.

"You don't remember me," Gainer said. "I can see that. What will you have to drink?"

A drink had the appeal of a cyanide capsule. Polly plunked down on a couch and drew up her legs and Dancey could have cried out in envy. If only he could lie still for a bit, take a little nap, he could face this confusing situation.

"Be seated, son. Bourbon?"

Dancey sat in a Renaissance chair in that opulent room and took the drink Gainer prepared for him.

"I remember the day I heard about your father," Gainer said, lifting his glass in a toast. "A great loss."

"Are you still with International Oil?"

Even as he asked the question, Dancey recognized its absurdity. Gainer had to be at least seventy. Nevertheless, he was surprised by the old man's laughter. He sat down across from Dancey, holding his drink in a great slack spotted hand, and laughed until his eyes were wet.

"Well, now, that's not quite the direction in which the relation went, son. I always thought of them as being with me. But you may have a point. I was bought out. Yessir. They bought and I sold and here I am living like a prince while other men dig in the ground for fossil fuels. Fossil fuels!" he repeated with a roar. "Well, oil fueled this old fossil, I can tell you that. Yessir."

"Don't I get a drink?" Polly asked petulantly.

"Godamighty, of course you do. Time was when ladies had to sneak off to the pantry for the Lydia Pinkham's. But then you weren't raised to be a lady, were you, Polly?"

"I wasn't raised to be anything."

Gainer gave her a watery drink and said to Dancey, "Your mother was a lady. What's become of her?"

"She married again."

"Ah."

"And again."

"She was a beautiful woman."

Gainer seemed genuinely interested when his questions drew forth Dancey's academic background. The old man allowed that he had an interest in the Middle Ages himself and Dancey remembered the parchment in the foyer.

"A beautiful thing, isn't it?" Gainer said. "I have a number of items that would interest you."

"I'm surprised you can get hold of things like that."

"Sometimes I surprise myself," Gainer said, but his grin faded swiftly. "The private collection is coming to be regarded as a public crime. They make a man feel like a bandit because he has a love for things of the past. Sometimes you do have to be a bit of a bandit. Put 'em all in public places, that's the theory. Bullshit. That just makes them the private collection of some curator who didn't lift a finger to find the stuff."

There was a response to that, but Dancey was unequal to formulating it. The bourbon joined the luncheon wine in his bloodstream and he nodded in lazy acquiescence. Gainer warmed to his theme, generalized it, considered the world at large, grew angry.

"Madmen shooting up airports, kidnappings, terrorism, absolutely pointless violence. Dancey, it frightens me. We are in the midst of undeclared war."

Dancey stirred, about to mention that he had been there at the airport when Porres was killed, but Polly spoke first.

"If you go on about what's wrong with the world, you'll short out, Uncle Nate."

"Dancey, one reason I miss your father, I could talk to him. He had a grasp of things. He was an ambassador of his country, more so than those bastards on the Via Veneto. What kind of help could we expect from them if we fell into the hands of kidnappers or terrorists? They would begin by apologizing for capitalism. The best man we ever had over here was Clare Boothe Luce. It's a fact."

Polly was up, ready to go. Dancey rose to his feet. His head felt lighter than air, while his shoes seemed a deep-sea diver's boots. Gainer asked how long he would be in Rome.

"I'm doing some research at the Vatican Library."

"I envy you."

"Envy me? But you're here much of the time, aren't you?"

In a stage whisper, Gainer said, "The bastards don't like me. I have to fight tooth and claw to get in. They wear me down."

"I'm sorry to hear that."

"Did your university send you over here?"

It seemed best to leave his academic status vague. "I received a grant. A government grant."

"Don't apologize! It's your money, for Christ's sake. Take 'em for all you can."

"I'm sorry," Polly said in the car.

"He's a nice old guy."

"So many things bother him now. The government. The embassy. And terrorists. He is convinced that someone is going to kidnap me."

She laughed. Dancey did not. He yawned. Massacres and kidnappings paled to insignificance beside his need for sleep.

Polly said, "You look as if you're going to keel over." She increased the speed of the car, which was not soothing. She asked the name of his hotel. "Go up to your room, get in the sack and sleep till morning."

"Will I see you again?"

"We'll go on a picnic. There's a place I go to draw."

"You're an artist?"

"Call it therapy. I do watercolors. At the beach I only sketch. Tomorrow?"

He nodded. Tomorrow, the next day, soon. He liked Polly.

She turned onto the Via della Conciliazione and came to a stop by one of the pedestrian islands in the middle of the broad avenue. Behind, a blatting chorus of horns began. Polly lifted a defiant finger above her head. The gesture won Dancey beyond recall. Impulsively he leaned toward her. Her cheek was salty to his lips.

"Git," she said, slapping his thigh.

Git he got. The horns rose higher when he stepped out of the car. Oh, for the panache to give them the finger too.

5

"Signor Dancey. Signor Dancey."

The insistent voice of the desk clerk arrested him as he crossed the lobby, but when he looked back it was a youngish man in a seersucker suit just getting up from a chair who caught Dancey's eye. Dancey was still turned toward the elevator, and the promise of the bed in his cool room drew him so powerfully he felt that his body must be bent like a bow.

"You are James Dancey?" the young man said.

"Who are you?"

"I'm Carter from the consulate." He said this as if he expected to be contradicted. Carter looked to be in his very early twenties. "Welcome to Rome."

"I feel I've been here for days."

"There are several things about your grant that must be taken care of." Carter looked reproachful. "You didn't take a physical."

"There wasn't time."

"You can have it done here."

"What the hell for? To show I'm healthy enough to make the trip? Look, Carter, I am dead tired."

The elevator door opened and Ernesto Cielli stepped out, followed by Giuseppe.

"Here is Dancey," Carter cried.

"I see that," Cielli said, giving the young man a glance. He handed some money to the hovering Giuseppe, getting rid of him, and then proceeded to get rid of Carter.

"Give me the pouch, Carter. I'll handle this. There's no need for you to be absent from the consulate."

Carter seemed flattered by the suggestion that his absence might be noticed, but he handed the small leather pouch to Cielli with reluctance.

"We've got to open a bank account in your name," Cielli said to Dancey. "Think you're up to that?"

His stipend. Of course. Exhausted though he was, he needed money. In Washington, he had been provided with three hundred dollars in cash and that could not last long.

"Let's go."

Outside, having parted from Carter, they began to walk. Cielli looked at Dancey. "You seem to have gotten over your experience at the airport."

"Who was Porres?"

"He wasn't an American." Cielli seemed to think that settled that. Dancey thought of chauvinistic headlines. Plane crash in Ruritania, no Americans aboard.

"What was he?"

"That may never come out. Why did you take off?"

"The *carabinieri* found me. I didn't want to waste the day with them."

Cielli smiled. "Couldn't wait to see Rome? What did you do, just walk away?"

"I ran. Through the john, downstairs. I caught a bus just as it was leaving."

"You might have been shot!"

"Again."

Cielli thought about that, then nodded. It was nearly four o'clock; the heat was intense and muggy now, and the streets were relatively empty.

"God, I'm tired," Dancey said.

"This won't take long."

They entered a branch of the Banco di Roma and within minutes Dancey conceived a grudging admiration for Cielli. He was completely unimpressed by the suggestion that all personnel were at the moment so busy that the two of them would have to wait. Other

40

customers were straggling in, but the bank was far from back in business. Behind the huge counter, clerks were slumped at their desks, somnolent with pasta and wine. Cielli said they must see the *direttore* without delay.

"The *direttore* is not in."

"Then we'll wait in his office."

Cielli effortlessly flipped up a portion of the counter that served as a gate and nodded Dancey through. On the other side, gathering a convoy of agitated flunkies as they went, they headed for an office in the corner that seemed the center of power. A little man shaped like a beach ball and wearing an alpaca coat managed to plunge into the office ahead of them and announce their arrival. Cielli, it seemed deliberately, stepped on the man's heel. A shout of pain, a dancing about on one foot, but, more important, the emergence from behind his desk of the regal *direttore*.

"I am from the American consulate," Cielli said sweetly.

Indignation fled from the *direttore's* face and the clerks from the office as he shooed them away.

"Dr. Dancey wishes to open an account."

"A United States Government account?"

"Not directly." Cielli glanced at Dancey.

Ponzi, the *direttore*, could not disguise his interest in the pouch Cielli carried. He asked the two Americans to be seated. Cielli placed the pouch ostentatiously before him. Forms and papers were spread upon the desk. Cielli observed that Dancey would be working at the Vatican Library. Perhaps Ponzi knew Monsignor Roberto Nerone? Monsignor, Vatican, United States Government—clearly the *direttore* did not hit a parlay like that every day of the week. Reservoirs of efficiency that had needed only the probe of avarice to be tapped now revealed themselves. And then, after much signing and blotting, came the solemn moment.

"How much do you wish to deposit?"

Cielli undid a fastener on the pouch and spread the opening wide. The hand he plunged into it had the span of a pro basketball player's. When he withdrew it, he held a bundle of American currency of large denominations. He took another packet of dollars from an inside pocket.

"Fifty-five thousand dollars."

Ponzi could not repress a cry of delight. He translated the sum into lire, a currency falling steadily against the dollar. Another cry of delight. Dancey felt a bit like cheering himself.

When they left the bank, Dancey had a passbook in his breast pocket and Cielli carried with noticeable nonchalance a depleted leather pouch. Their passage was attended by the *direttore* himself and such of his subordinates as could attach themselves to the parade. Thus had Roman legionnaires returned from the provinces in a better time.

"You understand the purpose of the money, Dancey? Five thousand is for you, the rest is the government's contribution to some project that you understand and I do not. Very hush-hush." But the mocking expression in Cielli's eye suggested that he knew a good deal. "You will dispense money only on my direct orders."

"I'm glad it was you rather than Carter with me at the bank."

"Is that any way to speak of a fellow Georgetownian?"

"You're kidding."

"School of Foreign Service. It's a sure ticket."

"Did you go through there too?"

Cielli's smile suggested dyspepsia. "I am only a part-time diplomat, Dancey. Think of me as a concerned citizen, a businessman whose services are occasionally asked and willingly given."

"Carter wasn't serious about my taking a physical, was he?"

"I don't know if he was. I am. I want you to have one." Cielli paused. "The main point is a cholera shot. It won't take long."

"Please. Not today. I couldn't pass a physical now." But it was the mention of the shot that decided Dancey.

"Okay. I'll make another appointment for you. The doctor's name is Lancia. His office isn't far from your hotel."

"Thanks for the money."

"Tell me, Dancey. What's it for?" Cielli was whispering.

"Very hush-hush."

Cielli's laughter suggested that Dancey had just successfully passed a test.

6

The following morning Dancey entered Vatican City by way of the Via di Porta Angelica, a normal, noisy, traffic-congested Roman street which was not getting any sun at that hour. The guards at their posts were not all that different from the traffic cops one sees about Rome. A steady stream of automobiles entered the gate. One guard stood astride the walk, blocking Dancey's way, though not menacingly. Dancey told him what he was there for and was asked for his papers. He brought out some of his documentation. The guard compared the photograph and its subject more than perfunctorily. He returned the papers and stepped aside to allow Dancey to pass.

There was no immediate change after he had gone by the guard. He still walked along a fairly narrow street. On his right was the Vatican Post Office, the ultimate despairing recourse of the Roman defeated by the government mail service. Nothing changed and yet everything had changed. Dancey tended to be affected by crossing any border. Driving from the District into Maryland called for some celebratory rite. He told himself, trying to reduce his sense of awe, that this was more on the order of entering Disneyland, but of course it did not work. His knowledge of the popes was spotty, to say the least; like most non-Catholics, he tended to take Alexander VI, the Borgia pope, as typical—venal, carnal, simoniac—but of course he suspected that it was Alexander's uniqueness that had brought attention on him. The sense of being simultaneously in the present and the past which had been with him since his arrival in

Rome intensified when he entered Vatican City. Here there was a continuity between Then and Now lacking in the larger city, something more than the mere physical juxtaposition of different times. There was a tradition here that began to be obvious as he walked along, following the guard's directions. The papal arms, fashioned of hedges and flowers, appeared upon the lawns. The size and appearance of the buildings changed. Nothing on this street at this point was particularly old; he would have guessed that these buildings had been erected in the last century or so. But then he passed through an archway and came onto a large gravelly parking lot and, turning to his right, saw the entrance of the Biblioteca Apostolica Vaticana. Behind him now, looming high, though not as high as the great dome just beyond it, was the building in which the pope has his apartment, both asparkle in the morning sun. The sound of tires crunching on gravel brought him down to earth again.

Security inside the library was no more tight than at the gate. There was one of the glass-enclosed booths one sees in the foyers of public buildings in Europe and the usual officious man peering out of it. On the staircase which led to the *sala di studio*, a uniformed guard stood, but there was an Italian indolence in his stance.

Dancey produced his papers, but the man in the glass enclosure wanted only his identity card. He examined it at various distances from his eyes, he turned it over and over as if it might develop a third side, then rose to his feet. He came out of his cage and crossed the hall, his heels noisy on the marble floor. Halfway across, he stopped and looked back. His gesture indicated that Dancey was to go with him. The guard on the staircase followed all this with lounging curiosity. His job must be very dull if this could interest him. Dancey followed his guide a short way down a corridor, where he was abandoned on the doorstep of an office when the flunky's knock was answered and the man disappeared inside with Dancey's card. He turned it over to a broad, bald man with a great moon face. The face kept rising over the shoulder of the flunky, who stood in front of the desk, kept rising, then setting, until finally it rose for good and the man waddled across the office to the doorway.

"Dr. Dancey, welcome to the Apostolic Library. My name is Strommer. Ulrich Strommer. Dr. Ulrich Strommer, of course."

"Is something wrong?"

"You mean this delay? Not at all. Our personnel . . ." He thought better of it. "I am to introduce you to the subprefect. Did not Nerone tell you this?"

"I am obliged."

"Obliged?"

Nothing brings home to one the oddities of one's native tongue like trying to avoid colloquialisms with a foreigner. "Grateful."

With understanding, Strommer bared his teeth, in a smile: they were set in his gums separately and imperfectly. He could have spat between any two of them, if spitting had been his game, as clearly it was not. Here is a man, Dancey thought, whose life is defined in terms of the most arid aims of scholarship; the air he breathed would be the dry, dust-filled atmosphere of books. Did he even know or care about what was going on among his contemporaries mere miles from where he stood? Dancey doubted it. Events would have to get into the past before they became real for Ulrich Strommer.

"Nerone has told you how confidential our work is?"

"Yes."

"Say nothing to the subprefect. Nothing."

Dancey nodded. Strommer did not fill him with confidence, but he supposed Nerone knew his man.

"This way," Strommer said.

He pushed aside the staircase guard when they got to him. A moment of hesitation as he glared at the steps, and then he began to ascend. His breathing was more audible now, a puffing, protesting exhalation, and Dancey wondered if the man would make it. Strommer, ageless, baby-faced, could have been forty and he could have been sixty. In either case he had too much weight on him for these stairs. Climbing them was probably the only exercise he got, and judging from the way he had eyed them from the bottom, he did not go up them any more than he had to.

"Have you been here before?" Strommer asked, each syllable a separate puff. Dancey was reminded of the Gregorian chant parchment in Gainer's foyer.

"No, I haven't."

Dancey realized later that he had just conferred on Strommer the delight of being the one to show a newcomer the main reading room.

On the second floor, the hush was already palpable in the hallway. There were runners on the floor to muffle footfalls. They went through glass-paned swinging doors into the great *sala di studio*. Strommer stepped aside theatrically so that Dancey could have an unimpeded first view of the room. Directly before him was a massive marble statue of Leo XIII, the patron of the Thomistic revival, and at the far end, a matching statue and one that in sheer avoirdupois and solidity would have rendered Leo insignificant if they had been placed side by side, was the symbol of Catholic learning, St. Thomas Aquinas. The room was lined with books, the shelves rising to the bottoms of the vast windows which rose above them. Tables, places for scholars and, to Dancey's left, the inevitable library counter, behind which a little priest was observing Dancey's reaction. He had passed some test. If the test was to be impressed by that room, Dancey did not see how anyone could fail it.

"This is Father Jacques, the subprefect," Strommer said in English. Jacques. Strommer. Dancey realized how international this library, this city, was. Jacques' handshake was the limp European token touching.

"*M. le professeur,*" Jacques said. "*Je m'excuse, mais je ne peux pas parler anglais. Vous parlez italien, peut-être?*"

"*Mais oui, mon père. Ou francais, comme vous voulez. C'est tout à fait égal.*"

Strommer, whose Italian had been on the same order as Dancey's, seemed to squeeze himself with delight. An American who knew languages other than English! Dancey felt that he was getting off on a good foot here. It was agreed that they would speak Italian,

46

after Strommer had playfully suggested that German be their lingua franca and Dancey had entered into the fun by agreeing to that *auf deutsch*. Strommer had made the suggestion somewhat wistfully. Perhaps he had not been joking. Jacques said that their exchange should really be in Latin. No doubt both he and Strommer knew Latin as a spoken language—it functioned for Catholics not only as the incredibly involuted closet Latin of papal documents, but also, at least until recently, as the language of instruction in seminaries and pontifical universities, certainly those in Rome. For Dancey, Latin was something that existed only on the page, and he knew how difficult the transition from a reading to a speaking knowledge of a language can be. And vice versa. He had spoken French before he could read it and could not believe the difference when he first began to study it in school.

"Dr. Dancey has received a grant from his government to continue the research he began in preparing his doctoral dissertation," Strommer informed Jacques.

"Your thesis?" Jacques asked.

Dancey gave a résumé of the argument of his dissertation, a proof that the anonymous Parisian master whose quodlibetal questions he studied had been wholly unaware of the controversy over essence and existence.

"Then he must have taught at Paris before Aquinas," Jacques said.

"But there is internal evidence that he was a contemporary of Thomas and, indeed, survived him. There are unequivocal references to William of St. Amour."

Jacques frowned. "A misguided man. A bad man." Jacques was a Franciscan and William of St. Amour had likened the newly formed mendicant orders to the Antichrist. Clearly the insult was not centuries old for Jacques. Like Strommer, he no doubt lived in a timeless vacuum where all arguments are contemporary.

"And this is your first visit here?" Jacques said, quelling his righteous anger.

Dancey said that it was.

"Then we must give you a small tour."

Jacques led Dancey and Strommer through a door which was set in the wood paneling of the wall in so masterful a way that Dancey had not detected its presence until the little priest slipped a key into what seemed a flaw in the woodwork and opened the door to reveal a small room. Strommer made it through all right, although Dancey would not have bet on it when the fat librarian approached the opening. Dancey followed him inside and Jacques, bringing up the rear, pulled the door shut after himself. The room they were now in had rough stone walls and two small square windows, streaked and dusty in the morning sun. In the center of the room, as if it should have been encircling a baptismal font, a plinth, something, was a curved wrought-iron fence. What it enclosed was a hole in the floor. Or so at first it seemed. The hole turned out to be a stairwell with stone steps which twisted down into the darkness below. Jacques produced a flashlight and led the way.

Below Dancey was the beam of the flash, which jumped pointlessly around as if Jacques did not really need it; above him was the great puffing presence of Ulrich Strommer. They went down what Dancey imagined to be two flights before he heard a door opening below. When he reached the bottom of the steps, Jacques awaited him in a brightly lit, spotless room.

There was no darkness here, if Dancey had expected it; no moisture, no sense of natural atmosphere. Humidity and temperature were carefully controlled and the reason, in a moment, was apparent. All about them, in their special cases and containers, was a first inkling of the treasures of the Vatican manuscript collection.

As reverently as if he were saying Mass, Jacques brought out a great leather folder, placed it on a trestle table and opened it. Strommer and Dancey flanked the little priest like acolytes. Embossed on the cover of the folder was the catalog number of the manuscript it contained. It was a psalter done in the formal Gothic cursive, or so Dancey guessed. His guess was right. It had been four years since he had done any paleography, but knowledge is an adhesive thing. He felt it all coming back.

The manuscript dated from the fifteenth century. The next thing Jacques brought out was a commentary by St. Augustine on John's Gospel done in Caroline minuscule. Early ninth century. Gingerly Dancey put out his hand and touched it. It was like establishing contact with a scribe who had been dead for over a thousand years. He was reminded of the time he had entered the chapel at Aachen and stood under the great iron candelabrum in Charlemagne's chapel. A reeling vertigo, a sense of the reality and unreality of time, time asserting itself and being negated by space. The same coordinates that contained him had once contained the Holy Roman Emperor. Dancey could date the beginning of his passion for the Middle Ages from that moment. So too, now his hand lay on the parchment that had once supported the hand of the man who had inscribed these beautifully simple lines. None of them spoke. Jacques and Strommer seemed to sense what he felt and Dancey had a new respect for them both. Like physicians who become inured to pain and sickness, like priests who become too familiar with sacred things, it would have been understandable if Jacques and Strommer had grown blasé in proximity to such marvels. But they seemed as dumbstruck as he was.

"They're beautiful," he said. "How amazing that they should have been preserved."

"Amazing, yes. Miraculous." Jacques brought his hands together as if in prayer. "The mind finds it difficult to comprehend the contingency that lies behind the survival of such things. Here. Elsewhere. Scattered through Europe in national and municipal libraries, there are such manuscripts. Increasingly in your own country too. But nearly always, as is right, they are available to competent scholars. How does one put a value on such things? Yet there are individuals who wish to trade in them, to buy and sell them, to own them! To want such things for oneself is incredible. The private possession of objets d'art is an affront to mankind. When it comes to things of culture, we are all socialists."

Dancey shared Jacques' sense of the unfittingness for any one person to claim private ownership of such treasures. Paintings, sculpture, incunabula, manuscripts: they are a common patrimony.

But there seemed to be a special tone in Jacques' voice when he referred to America, perhaps the usual Gallic disdain of the lost continent. Of course tycoons, or the children and grandchildren of tycoons, had amassed private collections, but these, in the fullness of time, were bequeathed to the public. Nor were they, when private, wholly inaccessible. Often it was the private collector who assured that items were recognized as valuable, as part of the common patrimony. There was a place in all this for men like Nathaniel Gainer. Not that Dancey meant to argue the point with Jacques.

"So vulnerable," Dancey sighed.

"Here they are kept with great care."

"Yes," Strommer agreed. "And yet, how do you say it, Dr. Dancey, a stone's throw away—and how significant that phrase is—a stone's throw away events are taking place which jeopardize collections like this one. Collections of the unique. What is to be done? A copy of a painting, a photograph of it, any reproduction, is simply not the painting. The same is true of sculpture and coins and other artifacts. No more is a copy of a manuscript that manuscript. Yet the manuscript is in a separate class. They are not simply precious objects, irreplaceable things. They have a content and a message. And that can be preserved on film."

"As at your St. Louis University," Jacques said to Dancey, turning his back to Strommer. "There was great resistance to that project. The Romans—well, they are Romans. To them it is inconceivable that anything could be safer elsewhere than in Rome. Incredible. They know the history of the city as well as you and I. Nonetheless, resistance was overcome. I helped to overcome it. In the usual way. The Holy Father himself said it would be done and of course it was done."

"A great achievement," Strommer puffed.

"Yes." But Jacques was frowning now. "In the minds of some, that was a precedent. If once, why not again and again? But that is not the way things work in Rome. There were those, Ulrich among them, who suggested we make another complete copy of our manuscript holdings. Another!"

"Now, Father," Strommer said, glancing at Dancey. "There is no need for us to argue the matter again. The die is cast. You won. That is an end to it."

"I did not want to triumph over anyone," Jacques said gently. "You know it was not that, Ulrich."

"I know."

It was clearly important to Jacques that his motives be pure. Strommer had conceded too swiftly that they were. Did the priest himself doubt the reasons for his opposing the microfiche project?

"Not at all," Strommer said, when they had worked their way upstairs and downstairs and were seated in his office. "He is more than a scholar. He is a holy man. I would not say that of many men, not even priests. No, he is convinced that the St. Louis reproduction is all prudence requires of us against the vagaries of fortune. To make another would indicate an insufficient trust in providence, as if we thought it depended on us alone."

"Then he thinks the microfiche project has been dropped?"

"Yes." Strommer pulled at the corners of his mouth with pudgy fingers. "It is painful to me to deceive the subprefect. But I am convinced, though I am not a holy man, that in these times we would be derelict not to make another copy of our manuscripts."

"How can it be carried out if Jacques opposed it?"

"It will be difficult."

One of the appeals of Nerone's request had been that it transcended in importance the usual human tasks, yet here Dancey was caught up in a struggle between two camps. Such a project should command universal assent.

"Can't the microfiching be done here?"

Strommer regarded him mournfully. They had reached a sensitive point. The fat man rose from his chair and inhaled and exhaled his way across the room to the door. He shut it firmly and returned to his chair.

"No. Not here. That is why we have need of you, Dr. Dancey. I will not go into all the details. Some you will receive from Nerone. The manuscripts will be taken from the library, photographed and returned. It will be your task to take them and to bring them back."

51

"My God!" Dancey thought of the manuscripts he had just been shown by Jacques, the exquisite formation of letters, the illumined initials, their age. They were quite literally priceless. There was simply no replacement should one be lost. "But how?"

"You will walk out with them."

"Is that possible?"

"Were you searched when you came in?"

"No."

"No. The full responsibility for the security of the library is with the library itself. It is impossible for someone to have access to manuscripts without permission. He is seldom even left alone with them. The user of a manuscript cannot leave the library until it has been returned to its proper place. We have never once had a manuscript stolen."

"How am I going to get them out?"

"Permission to use manuscripts is given by the prefect, the subprefect, and myself. The prefect is actually never bothered with such matters. As for Jacques and myself, we have total trust in one another." A shadow passed over the moonlike surface of Strommer's face. "I shall be abusing his trust."

"Is is really worth it?"

"I put the same question to you. Do you find it inconceivable that this political fiction of an autonomous state should be overcome by events? I do not. No more do I think that the library of St. Louis University is invulnerable. You will say that lightning does not strike twice in the same place. But there are kinds of lightning which are designed to strike twice if they strike once. I would like to have Jacques' faith. But I am only a weak and very fat layman. Risks bother me. Responsibility weighs heavily upon me. I ask myself, what would my life be like without the treasures I handle every day? Nothing. Can I then fail to take precautions that may be the sole assurance that other men, in later centuries, will have the same privilege as I?"

It made sense to Dancey. It had made sense the first time, over dinner with Nerone in the Café di Napoli in Washington.

"Does Jacques carry more weight than the prefect?"

"You will find that in the Vatican it is often the second in command who is truly in command. Perhaps it is so in all bureaucracies. The prefecture is more or less an honorary position."

"If the prefect authorizes the removal of a manuscript, it is legal, is it not?"

Strommer thought about that. "Technically, yes. But we shall be removing manuscripts for a purpose that has not been approved by the Holy Father."

"Does he disapprove?"

"It was not thought expedient to take the matter to him."

"Would he have disapproved?"

Thought caused Strommer's face to sag, as if the flesh were melting. He nodded. "With the Holy Father, Jacques' view would prevail."

"That puts me in a dangerous position."

"It puts us all in a dangerous position," Strommer said, puffing a bit. "That is why we must test our procedures and see that they work. We shall run through them a few times. After we have made a certain number of microfiches, you will take them to the States, where they will be sealed and stowed."

"And I get my instructions from Nerone?"

"That is right. He wanted you to check in here, to meet Jacques, to establish yourself as a working scholar. A place has been assigned to you in the *sala di studio* where you can pursue your own research. Each day, shortly after noon, you will leave the library. Guido will hand you a package."

"Guido?"

"The man in the glass booth."

"Does he know . . . ?"

"It is good to make use of innocent intermediaries, unwitting instruments." Strommer might have been reciting an axiom.

"So every day I get a package from Guido."

"Yes. Because every day you will leave it with him when you come in."

"Ah. And during the course of the morning . . . "

"Exactly. You see how simple it all is, inside the library."

Dancey rose. "And outside is Nerone's concern?"

"Yes." The word became a sibilant hiss accompanying Strommer's getting up from his chair.

"Where is Nerone's office?"

"Monsignor Nerone is just down the hall. Why do you ask?"

"I suppose I should stop by there."

"No!" Strommer's voice was full of alarm.

"But how will I find out what I'm to do after I leave here unless I talk to him?"

"He will come to you. It is imperative that you never be seen speaking with Monsignor Nerone. Indeed, I shall not introduce you to him now, though that is the usual procedure for scholars. Nor will you and I speak like this after today. We shall see one another about, but there will be no *tête-à-têtes* between us."

Strommer spoke with great urgency. Dancey felt that he had just made some terribly importunate suggestion. He assured Strommer that he would be the soul of discretion. Not even his hairdresser would know for sure, he added. A mistake. While he attempted to explain the remark, Strommer frowned and rubbed his bald head. He never did understand. It was a lousy way to end the meeting, but Dancey felt it best to quit while he was only one unfunny punch line behind.

7

There were two messages waiting for Dancey when he came back to his hotel. One, from Cielli, informed him of an appointment with the doctor. That damnable physical. The second message was from Nerone and asked Dancey to join the monsignor for lunch at Trattoria Posti. Dancey cursed the caution that had prevented him from talking to Nerone at the library. He had left the library early, shortly before noon, anxious to have as much time with Polly as possible. If he joined Nerone now, it would be at best an hour, at worst two, before he could get away. He decided to ignore the note. Nerone could wait.

Nerone was waiting in his room.

He looked a bit like the Lincoln Memorial sitting there, his arms on the arms of the chair, a mournful countenance, robes draped around his legs in a monumental way.

"You seem surprised. I left a message."

"It said to meet you at the Trattoria Posti."

"Did it?" He waited for Dancey to read the message again. "This does not bode well for your ability to carry out instructions precisely."

The point was too fine a one to waste time on. Besides, Dancey was eager to get this session over with.

"I won't be able to have lunch with you, I'm sorry to say. I already accepted an invitation."

Nerone did not like it. He demanded to know who Dancey's luncheon partner was. That it was an old friend did little to

sweeten the monsignor's disposition. He reminded Dancey that he
was not in Rome to renew old acquaintances.

"It *is* an old acquaintance?"

"Actually, she's rather young."

Nerone's blank expression was that of a man for whom the
promptings of the flesh do not exist. "Did you telephone the
American consulate?"

"They sent a man here."

"Did you open the bank account?"

"Yes."

Nerone's manner brightened. No doubt it was a relief to know
that additional funding for the microfiche project had arrived. He
got to his feet.

"Very well. You will want to be getting to your young lady. Let
us get down to business. The route you took from the library today
is the one you must take every day. Exactly the same route. And
you must mimic exactly the carefree manner in which you walked.
No tension. No furtiveness. No looking behind. Nothing to suggest
that you are carrying something valuable. Rome is a nest of thieves,
pickpockets, purse snatchers, incredibly bold. And they have a
sixth sense in discerning worthwhile prey."

"Were you following me?"

The corners of Nerone's mouth twitched, then were still. "You
were being followed. More accurately, you were observed. This
will always be true on your trips to and from the library. It is a
security precaution. You will never be entirely on your own."

"That's a relief."

"Yes."

"Where do I take the manuscript?"

"Here. To your room. Where you will wait." There was a knock
on the door. "Until there is a knock on the door." Nerone crossed
the room and opened it. Giuseppe came in. He seemed to wait, like
a dog, for praise from Nerone. "Well timed," the priest said. To
Dancey he said, "Go with Giuseppe. Since you are not interested in
lunch, I will say good-bye."

Giuseppe held the door for him and Nerone swept out. After he

56

had closed the door, Giuseppe said, "We can speak Italian?"

"Of course."

Giuseppe looked at his watch. He continued to look at it. Several minutes went by. "Let's go."

They went past the elevator, past the marked stairway to a flight of stairs at the back of the building. It was narrow and airless and needed paint. The saddled stone stairs must have dated from the building's original construction, but were now a passageway for servants. Giuseppe's bald head glowed in the imperfect light as he led the way down.

On the ground floor, Giuseppe paused and indicated a closed door. It was his room. He seemed proud of it. Was it a privilege to live in the hotel? Apparently. Dancey lifted his brow in congratulation. Giuseppe's attention shifted to an outside door. It was open. He stood in it, drawing Dancey next to him.

"We cross to that building. Walk quickly and keep close to the wall. There is no danger here."

Danger? Dancey looked at him. Giuseppe seemed perfectly serious. Did the little porter even know what they were engaged in doing? He could imagine Nerone telling him some impossibly romantic story of what Dancey was up to. If there were not a priest involved, Giuseppe might have been led to believe that Dancey was keeping a rendezvous with a lady. Had aristocrats devoted themselves to impressing their servants? He could believe it.

Giuseppe patted his arm and stepped outside, keeping to the wall, moving swiftly. He might have been under fire. All the scene lacked was the chatter of machine guns. Plunging after Giuseppe, Dancey felt that he had reverted to childhood. He had a mad impulse to zigzag, the better to throw off the aim of those trying to gun him down. The bastards. They wouldn't get him. Giuseppe had arrived at their destination and held the door open for him.

The yard had been sunny, the building he entered was dark and, when Giuseppe closed the door, wholly devoid of light. Dancey sensed that Giuseppe had gone deeper into the darkness. He put out his hand and yelped. He had touched another hand.

A stone hand. A hand on which a stone bird sat. It was the hand of St. Francis. At the sound of Dancey's yelp, Giuseppe had turned on a flashlight. It filled and blinded Dancey's eyes and went away. It was when he opened his eyes that he saw the statue of St. Francis.

"What's wrong, signore?"

"Nothing."

"Relax. St. Francis watches over you."

It was a nice thought. Jacques was a Franciscan. Would the patron saint of his order watch over someone engaged in deceiving Jacques?

The flashlight went off. Dancey now had some sense of where they were. It was a garage-sized shed with a dirt floor. Giuseppe was on the far side. A crack of light had appeared between double doors.

"Come," Giuseppe called. Dancey joined him, going soundlessly over the dirt floor. The odor of garlic led him to Giuseppe.

Giuseppe pushed open the door and they emerged blinking onto a sidewalk. Giuseppe had closed the door and taken Dancey's arm, and now they merged into a flow of pedestrians. Perhaps if Dancey had not been blinking against the sunlight they would have looked like any other pair walking on the Borgo Santo Spirito. Suddenly Giuseppe cut across the street, pulling Dancey with him. They were headed for an open entryway on the opposite side. Through it was a cobbled courtyard jammed with cars. A man shot out of an enclosure inside the gate. Giuseppe waved him off.

"The *portiere*," he explained.

The man had taken several steps, then stopped, the flaps of his open coat subsiding. What a watchdog. But he had recognized Giuseppe and begun to nod.

Giuseppe threaded his way among the parked cars with Dancey in tow. Beyond the first courtyard was a second; Giuseppe came to a halt beside a nonfunctioning fountain in whose shadow three cats lay, watchful but lazy.

"The studio is on the third floor," Giuseppe said. He pointed. "There."

Someone in a lab coat appeared in the window. Giuseppe made

a gesture and the man disappeared. Moments later he emerged into the courtyard. A woman came out with him, she too wearing a lab coat, but she did not join them at the fountain.

"Luigi, this is Dr. Dancey."

Luigi was unprepossessing. His right eye wandered but his left made up for it in the intensity with which it studied Dancey. He might have been photographing the American. Finally he nodded and then, still looking at Dancey, bellowed, "Teresa!"

Teresa's lab coat reminded Dancey of the smocks worn by the street cleaners of Rome. Her hair was a haystack. Her skin was olive. Her black eyes were Spanish olives. Luigi told her who Dancey was and she brushed at her hair with the back of her wrist. The motion brought the smock against her body and the shapely line of her bosom was visible. Dancey guessed her to be thirty. Hose her down and groom her and she might address someone's concupiscence.

"Does the *dottore* want to see the lab?" Luigi asked Giuseppe.

"That isn't necessary." Giuseppe turned to Dancey. "You understand the process, don't you?"

Dancey did not understand it at all. His mind was on the picnic with Polly. Everyone seemed relieved at his disinterest.

"Nothing depends on your knowledge of the process," Luigi said. "Well, we know one another. That is the important thing."

That was it. They were dismissed. Which was fine with Dancey. The trip from the hotel had not taken much more than five minutes.

"Six minutes," Giuseppe corrected. "You will wait at the studio until Luigi has finished. Then bring the package back to the hotel."

The *portiere*, his smile revealing teeth like Scrabble tiles, stood up when they passed, but Giuseppe, with another wave, dissuaded the man from leaving his lair. They returned to the hotel as they had come.

In his room, washing, changing, putting on bathing trunks under his pants as Polly had suggested, Dancey thought of the instructions he had received, at the library from Strommer, and then from Nerone and Giuseppe. Important as the project was, he felt like a very small cog indeed. But it seemed wiser to be grateful that he had been chosen by Nerone. The microfiche project apart, he had received a research grant and that was a credit to be entered in his dossier. He wished that it had been unnecessary to tell Nerone of his date, but how else could he have got out of lunch at the Trattoria Posti? It had been pretty clear what Nerone thought of going on a picnic with a young lady.

ᛦ

Polly roared along the highway that led to Ostia and the Lido di Roma, the land flattening as they came closer to the sea. Cypresses, flowering trees Dancey could not identify, a perceptible alteration in the air. The top was down and Polly's hair, cut short though it was, was ablur in the wash of wind. Her chin tilted upward, her nostrils seemed to drink in the air, her small foot was heavy on the gas. Dancey was struck as he had been before by her foolhardy dismissal of possible danger. The road they were on, though of limited access, did admit traffic from both right and left. Among the more testing experiences is that of watching a vehicle inch onto a road along which you are hurtling at seventy-five miles an hour with someone else at the wheel. Like a problem in high school physics, one calculates at what point and how soon the two paths of force will intersect. Polly seemed not to calculate but simply to be devoid of doubt that, without her own least lessening of speed, the intruder would have cleared her path before any impact could occur. Dancey derived no comfort from the fact that she had been right thus far. A single mistake would be one mistake too many.

"Smell it?" Polly cried, sniffing like a rabbit.

"The sea?" He had to shout.

"Pollution. It's a crime."

She slowed down in order to pass through Ostia, and when she came to the shore road and the beach, turned right. The stench was overpowering now that the sea breeze cut across the car, yet the beaches were crowded with people. Ostia had always been a

61

favorite of Romans, a place to go during the lunch hour. Of course the long interlude from twelve to four and the new road facilitated this, but it was difficult to understand what the attraction was, given the condition of the beach. The odor was an oily one, as if some massive spill had occurred just offshore and sent its viscous assault together with dead sea life toward the beach.

"Ostia," Polly said. It was both an exclamation and an invocation. She seemed suddenly struck by how things change.

"Monica died here."

Polly looked at him, smiling vaguely, and turned back to her driving. She had not heard him. Monica, Augustine's mother, had died at Ostia when she and her son were on their way back to Africa after his conversion in Milan. Fifteen hundred years ago? Something like that. There was no way to escape such memories now. For much of the morning he had felt that he was taking exams in subjects all but forgotten and, to his delight, passing them. Talking with Jacques and Strommer had brought back more knowledge of medieval manuscripts than he thought he possessed and, with it, by oblique ties and crazy connections of memory, a great many pieces of quickly crammed lore were again at his fingertips. Hence the remark about St. Monica. He felt again the pedant's delight in isolated fragments of knowledge.

And he was glad that Polly had not heard him. It was pleasant to ride without the need for conversation, particularly now when she was on a road that might have been constructed with an eye to her pell-mell style of driving. But, with a kind of perversity, she drove more slowly now that speed was less dangerous. Dancey could not remember ever having been on this coastal road before. The area above Ostia was reminiscent of dozens of other developments created by the proximity of water: summer residences set back on gravel roads, the driveways covered by trellises on which vines grew. The smell of the sea was less objectionable now. He said so to Polly. It was no longer necessary to shout.

"And it gets better. Where we're going is perfect."

Perfect was not quite the word for the pebbly expanse of beach they came to, but in overwhelming compensation was the vast vision of the Mediterranean stretching out before them, polychrome in the blazing sun, green, blue, purplish, black, with the sky above a seeming mirror of the water. Not a cloud in the sky. Not a body on the beach.

"Don't ask me," Polly said when he asked why the beaches at Ostia were crowded and this deserted. "Look. There's my castle."

Dancey looked to where she pointed and stopped where he stood. They must have passed it on the road; it was in the direction of Ostia, but it had not been visible then. It was Norman and seemed to have been built on the very edge of the sea, squat, gray, powerful, impervious to attack from land or water. That bulky silhouette some hundred yards away conferred on the deserted beach the note of history. The Lido di Roma might have been a hundred other watering places, but this beach, with its brooding Norman castle, was itself alone.

Polly had loaded him at the car and now she began to take things from him, among them a multicolored striped terry-cloth blanket which, after several veronicas, she managed, assisted by the sea breeze, to spread upon the beach. She pinned down one corner of it with the picnic basket and took care of two others with her kicked-off sandals. Before taking the radio, she turned it on and abruptly the scene was violated by raucous music. Polly did not seem to share his aversion to the electronic wailing. She began to sway rhythmically to its far from subtle beat.

Dancey now held only a towel and a small square case with a handle in the center of its lid. Polly danced barefoot on the blanket, her half-closed eyes never leaving him, an odd smile on her full lips. She gave the impression of a pagan maid come through a time warp from a party thrown by Catullus, perhaps Horace's Lalage, *dulce loquens, dulce ridens,* or, since this was the twentieth century, just your average neurotic divorcee. Dancey was drawn to her, yet made wary by her apparent accessibility. She had hooked her thumbs in her skirt and begun to push down; the movement of her hips freed her from it. It drifted to the blanket like an ensign of defeat. Don't tread on me? Polly danced on it. Feet planted firmly now, only her torso moving, head tossing; her bouncing breasts brought memories of long-ago parties and bobbing for apples. It was fantasy fulfilled in the sunny afternoon, *l'après-midi d'un faune*. He loved it. Loved it and could not take it seriously. Polly's legs, long and tanned, emerged from the boxed hem of her blouse as if it were the only garment she wore. Enthralled, yes, but he was bothered by thoughts of amateur night at the topless bar.

Polly stopped moving, crossed her arms before her, took hold of the hem of her blouse, and stopped.

"You are wearing your swimsuit, aren't you, Jim?"

"You told me to."

"Then come on. I feel like an ecdysiast."

"I'll be the judge of that."

"Ha."

Her blouse lifted to reveal her swimsuit. Dancey dropped the case and towels and began working at his belt. He looked as if he hoped to tumble her then and there on that many-colored terrycloth blanket. But he was not half out of his trousers when she was on her way to the water, running in a lovely knock-kneed way. His clothes were a tangled pile when he went in pursuit.

The Mediterranean. The legendary middle of the earth, scene of a thousand dramas. But that afternoon, swimming out after Polly, Dancey was uninterested in history in its larger dimensions. Polly's antics on the beach had been definitely promissory of more than a brisk swim, a picnic lunch and so long, Dancey. Now that he had an idea of his task at the Vatican Library, the advantage of getting to know Polly better was obvious. He would be in Rome for months. Perhaps that was not much on the Mediterranean scale of time, but to a twenty-six-year-old groaning under the burden of celibacy, they stretched before him like a limitless vista.

Polly had swum with swift strokes perhaps forty yards out to sea before stopping. Her head bobbing in place, she waited for him. He was feeling the strain when he neared her.

"Puff, puff," she said. Water beaded her round, almost Slavic cheeks and her lashes were spiked, giving her eyes a penetrating look.

"I'm lucky to be alive. I was nearly assassinated at the airport when I arrived."

"You're kidding."

"Scout's honor."

"The terrorists?"

"Ottobre Quindici."

"Wow."

"So your uncle is right to worry."

"My uncle is often right." She looked at him from a corner of her eye. "He was right about my husband. And I assume he is right about you."

"About me? What did he say?"

"He says you are a genuine medieval historian."

"What gives me away, my sloping brow?"

"Oh, you don't know my uncle. He telephoned a friend of his at the Vatican Library."

"To check my story?"

"To verify his intuitions."

"The old sonofabitch. Does he always check people out?"

"Only friends and enemies."

"Which am I?"

Again a glance from the corner of her eye. She made a kissing sound with her lips. She lost her poise when he pressed his lips to hers. They began to sink. They went under, holding the kiss. When they emerged, it was to gasp for air.

Back on the blanket, she unpacked the picnic basket and his gaze traveled up the shore to the castle.

"Want to go up and take a close look later?" she asked.

"Is it empty or what?"

"No. People live there. There are apartments in the castle and a little feudal town. You have to drive in to see that."

"Why don't we?"

"Do you mean it?"

"Of course."

"Oh, good. I was afraid you'd think it dull. You know, just another old Norman castle."

"I *am* a medievalist," he reminded her.

"Someday I plan to live in that castle."

"You can let your hair grow and hang it out a window."

"Shut up and eat. Open the wine." ·

Unlike medieval manuscripts, Polly's Norman castle was made to survive wars. When they approached it later from the road, there was indeed a village: a small church, a twisting, dipping street lined with low stone houses in excellent repair and in current use, and then the castle itself, protected by a deep ravine across which a wooden gangway arched. Standing on the bridge, one could see that the castle was occupied. There was glass at the windows, and when they crossed over and peered in through a low one, they saw a room furnished in the modern mode. Apartments in the castle, indeed houses in the village, were, Polly said, considered an exclusive luxury. A very large amount of money must have gone into modernizing this.

"Fashionable weddings are held in the church."

"So this is where you want to live."

She looked around doubtfully. "It is a little cutesy, isn't it?"

"Oh, I don't know."

"Your face says it, Jim. And you're right."

"Polly, I like the place."

But, abruptly, her mood had changed. They went back up to the little street to where she had parked the car. In silence. The visit to the castle might have been a high point of the afternoon and it had turned into a depressant. Polly sought solace in speed and they raced back to Rome as if they had fallen hopelessly behind schedule.

What was their schedule? He had formed the thought that he would ask her out to dinner that night. The idea had lost some of its appeal when they left the castle and it did not commend itself when they passed Ostia and hit the open road. However, the farther they got from the sea, the sillier it seemed to permit a vagrant mood to spoil their day.

Once in Rome, they became snarled in a massive traffic jam

along the Tiber. As they inched along, he asked if she had plans for the evening.

"Would you like to see my pied-à-terre?" she asked, brightening.

"Where is it?"

"Let me surprise you."

Why not? Sun spilled into the open car. His arm angled out the window looked bronzed, the hair silvery. He became aware of envious glances from other motorists. Polly was an attractive girl with her feathery black hair and petulant profile, working her way through traffic with the best of them. Remembering how that morning he had chatted with Jacques of Caroline Minuscules, Dancey felt like a schizophrenic, but perhaps his afternoon was not all that distant from the hopes of scribes who had copied manuscripts in monastic scriptoria centuries ago. It was not rare to find at the end of a manuscript a sudden effusion from the copyist, often a prayer of thanksgiving that the job was done, sometimes a hope for wine as reward. Dancey had been particularly struck by one valedictory flourish. *Detur pro penna scriptori pulchra puella.* A raunchy aspiration, a lovely lass as the writer's reward, but it was one Dancey found understandable. The flesh has always been the scholar's weakness, as if he must reel from one extreme of experience to the other, from the arctic of disembodied mind to the common equator of carnal indulgence. Polly might be just what the scribe ordered.

Her apartment was near the Piazza del Popolo, a center of sorts for artists; she was on the fourth floor and had a lovely balcony that gave an angled view of the square and was high enough for the carbon monoxide from the traffic below to dissipate. Pots filled with flowers and herbs were scattered about the balcony, there were chairs of canvas and wicker, a cat who resented Dancey's presence, and a welcome glass of beer. He sat sipping, looking down at the great piazza, which had become in these latter days a vast circular parking lot, and said what he hoped were appropriate things about the watercolors Polly brought out for his inspection. As amateur work it seemed all right. Later they ate in a restaurant in the piazza. They came back upstairs. Polly shooed the cat onto the balcony and they went to bed. The sound of car horns rose in the night and Dancey had the unnerving thought, as he strove to assuage the appetite of this surprising girl, that they were maneuvering through traffic, and not too well, a source of annoyance to the other drivers.

"Do you believe in God?"

"What!"

"I asked if you believe in God."

"I thought that's what you said."

They lay as earlier they had lain afloat in the Mediterranean, side by side, on their backs, staring upward. Her head seemed sunk in her pillow and her voice was almost that of a child when she asked that ultimate unnerving question. It was not something he would have feared being asked by Nerone, or even Jacques, trusting, he supposed, in the fact that they were professionals. For Polly to ask it just then suggested postcoital remorse and he wished that he had been less concerned for her feelings and left when he had wanted to, earlier. They had talked inconsequentially and made love and then lain enjoying the silence, or so he had thought, and he knew that he should be getting back to his hotel. It would not do to arrive at the library exhausted his first real day on the job. Apparently Polly had been lying there brooding in the semidarkness rather than basking in the afterglow of their efforts.

He said, "I don't know."

"What do you mean, you don't know?"

"It's not an easy question."

"Well, it's not one you can just shove aside either. It makes all the difference, one way or the other."

"Do you?"

Silence for a moment. "Yes. The less I act like it, the more I do. Funny. Do you realize we're surrounded by churches here? Two in the piazza, another just up the street, more as you go. To the east and west of us too. How many churches are there in Rome, I wonder."

"Plenty."

"Hundreds? A thousand? More? There are non-Catholic churches too, you know."

"I know. And a Protestant cemetery where the bones of Keats lie buried."

"Are you a Catholic, Jim?"

"Are you?"

"I don't know if I can be, after the divorce. I guess I am. Not much of one. I have to do something about that."

"Confession?" He imagined her telling some priest what they had done. He was not sure he wanted billing as her partner in sin.

"It's been a couple years since I've been. I used to go regularly. Every month. I don't know what I confessed. God knows I wasn't up to much in those days. It was a routine. If someone had asked me then if I believed in God, I would have reacted the way you did."

"How do you mean?"

"Embarrassed. Weren't you embarrassed?"

"I guess so."

"Funny."

She fell silent. He wanted out of there. A minute or so and then he could make some excuse and go. He yawned, forcing it; it seemed a way to change the subject.

"When your life disintegrates, like when you get a divorce, it's as though the earth opened up under you. What always supported you just isn't there anymore. But you figure there has to be something else, deeper down. You can't just float over nothingness. Otherwise anything goes."

"Dostoyevsky."

"Hmmm?"

"He said much the same thing. If God does not exist, anything is permitted."

"Did he believe in God?"

"Yes."

"If God exists, not much is prevented either."

He yawned again and sat up, putting his feet on the floor. He remained seated on the edge of the bed for a moment. Something coiled through his ankles and he cried out. Polly sat up and her breasts came into the light filtered from the street.

"The cat," Dancey said. He reached out and put his hand on her shoulder. She scooted across the bed and he took her in his arms. What a strange girl she was.

"Going?"

"I'd better."

She did not protest. They kissed. He dressed. Downstairs he had to walk for blocks before he found a cab.

9

The office of Dr. Piero Lancia was on the Borgo Santo Spirito and Dancey arrived there largely because Cielli came for him and drove him to the door. Dancey dawdled and did not get out of the car.

"What's wrong?"

Cielli's tone was impatient. Dancey decided not to say that he was in a weakened condition from a heavy date. It was so unlikely that he should be able to make such an excuse in truth that he did not want to lay it open to Cielli's scorn or derisive laughter. He opened the door and got out. Cielli did not drive away. There was nothing to do but go in.

Dr. Lancia's office was on the first floor of the building and his waiting room had the look of a salon rather than an office. The receptionist, middle-aged, blue-haired, with great pendant earrings, rose to greet him.

"Dottor Dancey?"

"Yes."

She sat, sighing as she did so, giving the impression of a subsiding balloon. Her hand fell to the phone, and when she lifted it, she fixed her eye on Dancey as if to render him immobile. She waited, her breathing audible. She and Strommer could have given a respiratory duet.

"He is here," she told the phone, then put it down.

A minute later, a young man in a white cloth coat appeared in the doorway. "Are you Dancey?" he asked in English.

The receptionist replied that this was indeed the American Dancey. She sounded as if she had just produced him from a hat before a hostile audience. Apparently his failure to show up for the first appointment had made her wary.

"Lancia," the young man said, bowing. "Come with me."

In his office, Lancia settled behind his desk, picked up a form and immediately began to read a list of ailments and diseases, in search of Dancey's medical history. The doctor read the list slowly, he seemed completely unhurried, but then his waiting room had been empty and it was Saturday. Dancey wondered if he had ever before known a physician to bother himself with the routine aspects of a physical examination. Increasingly on such occasions one was put into the hands of nurses and technicians, handed from room to room, from machine to machine, until, finally, one confronted a doctor armed with all the results. Lancia finished the list and asked Dancey to step onto a scale. After weighing him metrically, which Dancey found about as informative as learning how many stone he weighed, Lancia took his blood pressure. Either Lancia was extremely taciturn or he had no small talk. All this went on in total silence save for the wheeze of the rubber ball. Dancey's remarks, the usual nervous joking of the experimental animal, went ignored.

"Come with me," Lancia said.

Dancey was beginning to think that Lancia's English was exhausted by such phrases, but switching to Italian released no flow of conversation from the doctor.

They had removed themselves to an examining room, where Dancey stripped to the waist, sat on a table and was listened to by Lancia, who moved his stethoscope about on Dancey's chest and back with delicate curiosity.

"Inhale."

He inhaled. He exhaled. Lancia gave no indication of what he thought of what he heard. A more intimate examination followed, involving a falsetto cough.

"I will need some blood," Lancia said.

"Blood!"

"A small sample. Please be seated." He pointed toward a small table flanked by chairs.

"Is this necessary?"

The examination to this point had had a remote, even theoretical tinge to it, but Lancia's request for blood filled Dancey with fright. He had always been a coward when it came to any puncturing or intrusion into his body; he found uneasiness, let alone pain, intolerable. In the dentist's chair he quaked when there was nothing more menacing than a mirror in his mouth. The sound of a drill was sufficient to render him boneless with dread. He would confess anything rather than submit to the drill without Novocaine, and even with Novocaine he was so taut that it took him days to unknot his muscles after a dental appointment. Shots made him faint. It was a miracle that he had not been reduced to idiocy by the massacre at Fiumicino. But Lancia's request for blood brought back an especially embarrassing memory.

Three years before, Dancey, rising to an unheard of level of heroism, had agreed to give blood to replace that used by a fellow graduate student who had had an operation. When the day arrived, he would have called to break the appointment if the student, whose name was Marge, had not come to drive him to the clinic. She came inside with him too, thereby blocking his intention to feign illness at the last moment, to lay claim to anemia or hepatitis or any other ill that flesh is heir to, in order to have his heroism vetoed. When the nurse asked him if he had had any alcoholic beverages in the past twenty-four hours and he answered no, his last chance of lying his way out like a man was gone. Somehow more terrible than his cowardice was the thought of the girl learning of it.

And so he had been led away, put into a sort of astronaut's chair, been tipped back and asked for his arm. He offered it to the technician, a very young girl, a mere child, it seemed, obviously an amateur. How many patients had she lost? She tied a rubber tube about his upper arm, exerting pressure, brightly explaining that she was looking for a vein. Against his will, Dancey's eyes were drawn to his helpless arm and to the blue vein pulsing there. He watched with horror as she applied a surface anesthetic and then inserted the needle. For a moment, he thought he was going to make it. And then she turned on the motor. He saw the plastic darken with his blood. He felt, he knew, that he was going to be sucked dry. He screamed. Before they got the motor off and the needle out of him he had fainted. Twenty minutes later Marge helped him out to the car. He might have come as a patient rather than a donor.

All this flooded back into Dancey's mind in Lancia's examining room: the fright and the further fright that his first fright would be discovered. He crossed the room and sat. He allowed Lancia to take his arm. The doctor pricked Dancey's fingertip. A drop of blood appeared. Lancia squeezed the tip of the finger and the drop grew larger. He brought a glass tube to the wound and drew blood; it rose like mercury in a thermometer, and watching it, Dancey began to sway. He was perspiring. He felt faint. Lancia looked at him and smiled.

"There," Lancia said.

"Done?" The glass tubing was red with his blood. Lancia stood and walked across the room.

"Done."

Dancey's breathing returned to normal. The dampness of his body seemed only a healthy sweat. He was proud of himself. There had been nothing to it. Lancia was back. In his hand was a huge needle.

"Your cholera shot," he explained.

Dancey said nothing. His eye was on the tip of the needle, which seemed to grow in size as he stared. Lancia gripped his arm lightly. He thrust. Dancey tried to pull his arm free at the last moment. He started to rise. He crumpled to the floor.

He was in the reception room, sprawled on a sofa, still bare to the waist. The fabric of the cushions felt strange against his flesh. The receptionist looked down at him.

"Feeling better?"

"I'm sorry," he said pointlessly, as if he had spoiled her day.

She brought a glass and told him to drink. He drank. She told him to dress. He dressed. Lancia was nowhere in evidence. He felt a need to explain to the doctor, to tell him some saving lie. He was exhausted from travel, an insatiable female had worked her will on him, his mother had gone to a Bela Lugosi movie while pregnant with him, cholera ran in the family. But he was glad to be alone with the motherly receptionist. A tuft of cotton adhered to his fingertip.

"Drink it all," she urged, and he drained the glass like a good boy. "Better now?"

In the grip of bravado, he stood and began to button his shirt. He swayed with the room, kept the floor beneath his feet and tried to smile at the woman.

"Rest some more. You can sleep if you like."

Mocking laughter. His own. His voice was assuring her that he was fine, just fine. He found that he was leaving. At the door, he turned, intending to say that he would return and complete the physical, but all he could manage was a jaunty wave. He shut the door on her concerned babble.

The Borgo Santo Spirito offered a surrealist prospect; objects melded and floated apart, sounds made a separate world from colors. He put his hand against the building, to steady himself, and the stone felt porous, as if with the slightest pressure he could bury his hand in the wall. His room. His bed. Existence seemed summed up in that destination. It seemed too late to return to the reception room. By closing one eye, he managed to bring order into the street. A passer-by hesitated, then continued on. He must not make a spectacle of himself. The tuft of cotton still stuck to his finger. He held it before him, a badge of honor. He was wounded. He had donated blood. He moved off, aiming at a street lamp some distance away. When he reached it, he stopped. The traffic in the street had the unbroken look of a passing train. And then, across the street, he saw the garage doors from which he had emerged with Giuseppe. They seemed to be what he was looking for.

Crossing the street, aware of horns and brakes and irate voices, he was reminded of Polly weaving among the cars and he began to laugh. He showed his tufted finger to the world. He felt euphoric.

He felt invulnerable. He felt a car fender nudge his leg. He made it to the opposite curb. Leaning against a wall, he realized that he had collected a group of children. He dug in his pocket for coins and scattered them on the walk. It was like feeding birds. That odd maniacal laughter was his own. Strange. He settled against the wall. He would wait there until he felt better.

A minute later he was walking toward those garage doors. The children were gone. The door opened and he stepped into the darkness and shut the door behind him. A measure of clarity returned with nothing to see. He could not find St. Francis. He aimed himself through the dark and found the opposite door on the third try.

Crossing to the door of the hotel, he did zigzag. His life had become hurried and hush-hush. Western civilization rested precariously on his shoulders. He regretted that he had but two gallons of blood and immunity to cholera to give to his country. Up the ancient stone stairs, down the hall and into his room. He collapsed on his bed, the ultimate mistress, and was immediately asleep. The voice of Cielli whispered unintelligibly in the dark.

10

"Since you are a Thomist, you will want to see this." Strommer sounded like one of Santa's helpers.

"Monsignor Nerone has been telling my secrets," Dancey said.

Strommer opened a folio on the table before them. "MS Vat. lat. 9850, fol 2ra-89vb" was the legend. It was part of the *Summa contra gentiles* of St. Thomas Aquinas, running from Chapter 13 of the first book to Chapter 120 of Book Three. It was an autograph, actually written in the hand of Thomas himself. Dancey looked down at the double-columned parchment page and at the chicken tracks that had been made there *calamo currente*.

"The *littera inintelligibilis*," Strommer said reverently. "The unreadable hand. You will agree that it is well named. Can you make anything of it?"

Dancey leaned closer to study the script. From time to time, the marks seemed to assume familiar shapes, but then the hint was gone. It was completely opaque to him. He shook his head. Strommer got out a magnifying glass, directed it at the parchment, and a selected oval of script leaped toward Dancey's eye. It did not help to have the text enlarged.

"The man who succeeded in decoding Thomas's hand for our times went blind in the effort. He found that magnification was the only way."

If it was an exaggeration for Dancey to call himself a Thomist, he was student enough of Aquinas to be overwhelmed at having before him the very page on which the saint had written. It mattered little that he could not decipher the script. He knew that it was a species of shorthand, abbreviations of Latin words, as all manuscripts are. The transition from manuscripts to the printed page where the text of an author reads straightforwardly suddenly seemed to Dancey an immense journey, one fraught with possibilities of error and misinterpretation. The critical text, constructed from chosen readings from families of manuscripts, copies of copies, a tree with many branches, was in its way only an idealized guess, always open to correction. Thus, to have of a thinker of Thomas's stature *his* version of a text, one written in his own hand, was an inestimable boon to editors. It was not a matter of trying to reconstruct from a whole congeries of copies the putative original; the original itself lay before his eyes, the proximate standard of the printed text.

"It is priceless," Strommer breathed.

"Yes." The word seemed inadequate.

"I wanted you to see what your cargo would be."

"This!"

"Yes." Strommer's eyes went past him to the closed door as if he feared Jacques might overhear, but the little priest was in another part of the library, floors away from where they stood. "We have decided that the time has come to take real risks. Our routine is established now. We will all breathe much easier when manuscripts such as this one have been copied and returned."

Dancey felt anew the full dimensions of what he was engaged upon. The removal of these folios from the safekeeping and carefully controlled atmospheric conditions of the Vatican Library, if only for a few hours, seemed an impossibly risky undertaking. Strommer was turning the folio pages lovingly and Dancey had an impulse to withdraw from the project. He did not want to be responsible for something as precious as that Thomistic autograph, even for a few hours. But he said nothing. How different things might have been if he had.

"You must go to the *sala di studio* now. The rest is up to me. I will let you know when Guido has a package for you."

In the reading room, he paged through Froissart, surreptitiously watching the other scholars at their labors. An elderly woman at the end of his table sat surrounded by neat little stacks of notes, a book propped before her as she scribbled away. Her white hair was braided and arranged in a kind of coronet atop her head. Her skin was as smooth and dry as parchment. Her nose twitched as she worked. It is always difficult to tell about people in libraries. The crank and the genius sit side by side, indistinguishable in outward manner. That woman might be working on what would become a definitive work in whatever her field was. Then again, she could simply be amassing notes, putting off and putting off the evil day of composition. Whatever the case with her, there was something infinitely consoling about the reading room. One had the sense of everything in its place, a place for everything, all under control, every precaution being taken to preserve the contents of this magnificent library. Knowing what he knew, Dancey felt possessed of a guilty secret. He had the mad image of himself standing up and announcing to these shocked scholars that the autograph of Thomas Aquinas's *Summa contra gentiles* was even now being transferred to the porter's lodge in the lobby in preparation for an unauthorized departure from the Vatican.

At the end of the room, the great hulking marble image of Thomas Aquinas presided over these scholarly labors. A raised didactic finger seemed to counsel silence. Having actually touched the parchment on which the living hand of the saint had written, Dancey was less impressed than he had been by the image. On the hagiographical scale, the folio amounted almost to a first-class relic, while the statue did not rank at all.

Dancey was aware of heavy breathing behind him and turned to see Strommer standing there. The fat man's eyes flickered significantly. Everything was ready. Strommer turned and waddled from the room. Dancey remained seated, giving Strommer time to huff downstairs to his office.

The trip to the hotel was uneventful, though his nerves never quite believed it. When he came down the stairs, Guido called out to him and presented him with a large plastic briefcase, saying nothing as he did so. Dancey too said nothing, simply took the case, put it under his arm and sauntered from the building. He left Vatican City without incident, received the suggestion of a salute from the guard, turned right and proceeded through St. Peter's Square and continued on to the Columbus Hotel. It was that simple.

Until he got to his room and waited in vain for Giuseppe's scheduled knock.

Dancey sat in a chair and tried to prevent his knees from jumping. If he put only the ball of his foot on the floor, his knee began a rhythmic motor movement that caused the package to bounce about on his lap. He could stop this nervous activity only by putting both feet flat on the floor and leaning forward to exert pressure on his legs. Where in hell was Giuseppe? After several minutes, Dancey began to follow the second hand around the face of his watch. Around and around and around, but still there was no knock on the door.

He stared at the door panels as if willing Giuseppe to come down the hall and accompany him out the back way to the studio on the Borgo Santo Spirito. Ten minutes went by. Something was wrong. It had been impressed upon him that the essence of the procedure was precision without improvisation. Giuseppe was supposed to knock on his door within five minutes of his return from the library. He remembered the dramatic way in which Nerone's narration of the procedure had been punctuated by the actual knock on the door. And so it had been the first two times.

Pacing about the room did not help. He kept away from the balcony, fearful he might find the redhead next door sunning herself on the balcony a few feet from his own. She seemed to live in the sun and someone more vain than Dancey would have connected her presence with the possibility of his appearance on the balcony. The redhead was wont to lisp some banality about the weather or the city while staring at Dancey with smoldering eyes. All fine and good when he was off duty, as it were, but out of the question now.

Was he being tested? This was, after all, only the third run. Up until now everything had gone like clockwork. It made some sort of infuriating sense that Nerone would want to know how he would react if the procedure was altered without warning. He went to the bed, pulled back the spread and inserted the plastic briefcase under the sheets. Walking to the door, he looked back at the bed. The briefcase was clearly visible under the bedclothes. Before he could do something about that, there was a knock on the door. Giuseppe peeked in, a twinkle in his eye.

"Where the hell have you been?"

"Have you got it?"

"Of course."

"It will be a minute. Here."

Giuseppe thrust his hand into the room. It held a glass of beer. Dancey took it and the door closed.

What the hell was going on? He stared at the closed door and then at the foam on the beer. Drink me? He shrugged, brought the glass to his mouth and emptied it in two long draughts. Wiping his lips, he turned toward the bed. The manuscript.

He took two steps before the floor seemed to open beneath him like breaking ice on a not quite frozen lake. Gently, gently, he sank into the dark.

II

It was dark when he awoke, fighting his way to the surface of consciousness. His head felt like a balloon and he was surprised, when he brought his hands slowly to his temples, to find that it was the same size as it had always been. Feeling somewhat euphoric, he blinked, wondering why it was dark. When he brought his hands down from his head, his left hand settled on an arm. Someone else's arm. There was someone on the bed beside him. It seemed to be a man.

Dancey swung his legs off the bed and stood, but he did not achieve balance and stumbled and fell, hitting the wall with his outstretched hand. He got to his feet and groped along the wall, looking over his shoulder to where the bed was darkly discernible. This was not his own room, he knew that before he found the switch, turned on the light and saw that it was Giuseppe on the bed.

The room was Giuseppe's. The bed was Giuseppe's. The porter stared fixedly at him. Unblinkingly. Dancey started to say something, a facetious remark, his mind racing to find some acceptable explanation for the fact that he had woken up in bed with a middle-aged hotel porter, but he stopped before any sound emerged. Dancey's experience with dead bodies was limited, but he was suddenly certain that Giuseppe was dead. Surprisingly, this cleared his mind and calmed him. He went to the bed, avoiding Giuseppe's stare, and saw what looked like a wire around the porter's throat, drawing flesh in upon itself as if it were a device to correct the sagging skin of his neck. There was a bunch of keys visible on Giuseppe's belt and Dancey took hold of them and pulled. The belt would have to be unbuckled in order to free the keys. Dancey fumbled with the buckle, fighting the thought that this was insane. The door would now burst open and he would be discovered apparently groping the crotch of a corpse. The buckle unfastened and he slid the key container toward the middle of Giuseppe's body. The keys caught on the buckle; it was the wrong end of the belt to slip the keys off. This put him in a rage and he began to yank frantically at the belt. Giuseppe's body lurched and then rolled slowly off the bed. Dear God, what an inanimate sound it made when it struck the floor. Dancey had managed to keep his grip on the belt and he tugged and pulled, jostling the dead body of poor Giuseppe about, and then the belt whipped free. It snapped and struck the head of the bed and he lost hold of it. He watched it slither out of sight, taking the keys with it. Those keys now seemed something he must have, as if he had been unconsciously aware that his room key was not in his pocket. It was not. He discovered that now. He got down on his stomach and reached beneath the bed, slapping his hand about, in search of the belt. He found it and dragged it out from under the bed, but the keys were not on it. Maddened, he slid under the bed and found the keys.

When he was on his feet, the keys in his hand, he looked down at Giuseppe and was flooded with nausea. His mouth was furry as it had been at Lancia's and he no longer felt euphoria. He was going to be sick. He turned away from Giuseppe and bent forward, but he was unable to avoid his feet and was sick all over his shoes.

Finished retching, he began to cry. He was twenty-six years old but he stood there, his shoes and ankles sloppy with his own vomit, and cried like a baby. But a baby who was crafty enough to muffle the sound. It was not Giuseppe he wept for, it was not concern for the manuscript in his bed; he wept with his mind full of the indignity of having fainted in Lancia's office. His shame was the shame he had felt leaving the blood bank with Marge. He was a physical coward. The adjective did not help. How many kinds of coward are there? The kind he was saw that it would not do for

84

him to remain there in that room with the dead body of Giuseppe. He did not relish the thought of explaining what he was doing here, let alone what had happened to Giuseppe. His mind seemed to slide behind his eyes, threatening to go over some ledge, but he stopped it, secured it. He would not permit the thought that somehow he had risen from the floor, come down here to Giuseppe's room and choked the life out of him with that wire or whatever it was taking tucks in the skin under the porter's chin.

On his way to the door he passed a dresser. His eyes in its mirror were almost as expressionless as Giuseppe's. His hair was wild on his head, his beard matted. He looked drunk. He felt drunk. He felt drugged. He wet a towel at the sink and held it against his eyes, nearly swooning as he did so. He lowered himself onto Giuseppe's bed, thinking as he did so that the porter would have no further use for it. A sad thought, but it simply registered a fact. Were there family and friends to mourn for Giuseppe? At the moment, it was the fear of joining Giuseppe rather than sorrow for his passing that gripped Dancey. He had to assess the situation. What the hell had happened anyway? He had to get in touch with Nerone. If only his mind were clearer.

The soothing feel of the wet towel on his face was almost too much. He wanted to lie back on the bed, just for a moment, only a moment, a chance to close his eyes—but he knew that would be fatal. A knock on the door brought him into a sitting position.

"Giuseppe, are you there?"

For answer, Dancey grumbled in what he hoped was an acceptable imitation of Giuseppe himself. The man had been, after all, a bit of a martinet with the other employees.

"You're wanted at the desk. Hurry."

A grumble of assent this time, but Dancey got off the bed and moved quickly to the door and listened. A raincoat hung from a hook on the back of the door and behind it was a long black garment. It appeared to have red buttons. He had to get out of there. Every pore of his skin seemed to register separately on his brain when he opened the door and stepped into the hall.

The outside door was open and Dancey went to it, his head filled with the notion that he would dash out the back way and disappear forever. A child of five or six, a girl, was seated on a bench beneath a tree. She stared at Dancey. Her eyes moved from his face down to the mess of his shoes and trouser bottoms. Her expression changed slowly. Dancey smiled at her. At least that is what he tried to do. The effort brought a look of terror to the child's face. She leaped up and began to run toward the side of the building, calling in a shrill voice, *"Mamma, mamma."*

Dancey backed inside and went upstairs by the narrow staircase. He was halfway up before it occurred to him that his room might not be a haven, but he could not go down again, not with that screaming brat outside. A cry of desperation almost escaped him as he mounted the sunken treads. It seemed unfair that he could not have time to clear his head and think. The length and width of the hallway appeared immense when he emerged from the staircase. He was still holding Giuseppe's key ring, and when he got to his door, he fished forth a likely key but had trouble getting it into the lock. Was the door locked? It was. He rattled the knob, the sound louder than he would have expected. He had to get out of this corridor. The key slid into the lock then and a moment later he was inside with the door shut behind him. He leaned his back against it, his eyes fixed on his bed. It was a mess. The spread was pulled back, the sheets had been half torn from the mattress, the mattress itself was at an angle to the bed. There was no doubt that the package was gone. The Thomistic autograph that had been entrusted to him was gone.

There was the sound of voices in the courtyard and he staggered across the room and slumped into a chair. Giuseppe was being called for down there. And then, startled, Dancey recognized the authoritative voice of Roberto Nerone. He got up and moved closer to the door that gave onto his balcony, keeping out of sight of those below.

"He was in his room," someone was saying. "He answered when I knocked."

"Did you see him?"

Hesitation. Then, "No."

"He didn't open the door?"

"No."

"Go get him!" Nerone roared. "Break the door down if you have to. I want to see him."

Dancey edged closer to the window and looked down. Nerone's voice was still audible below, but he was speaking less loudly, in conversation with the menials from the front desk. He was turned away from Dancey and in any case his head was blocked from view by the balcony ledge. Did Nerone know what news he was waiting there to learn? Dancey was sure of it. Nerone knew what would be found when the door of Giuseppe's door was opened. And, when he found who was no longer there, he would know who had answered the earlier knock on the door. Dancey whirled and looked about his room. The bed? The armoire? The bathroom? Like a child, he was seeking a place to hide. But that was absurd. He had to get out of his room. He squeezed his hands in anguish and became aware of the keys he carried. Giuseppe's keys. And he thought of the room next door, the redhead's room.

It was an act of heroism to step into the hallway again. Dancey expected it to be swarming with porters doing the bidding of Nerone, seeking out the supposedly delinquent Giuseppe. He freed the key with which he had opened his own door, assuming it was a master key. It was. He turned the key, turned the knob, opened the door. There was no time for hesitation now. He stepped inside the room and closed and locked the door after him.

The room was in semidarkness, the drapes pulled across the French doors leading to the balcony. The drapes moved slightly, indicating that the balcony doors were open. A musky feminine smell pervaded the room. The bed was ajumble, dresses scattered over it, cast aside. Apparently the woman had been in the grip of indecision when she dressed to go out. For it was obvious that she was out. There was no sound from the bathroom and he had not been greeted by a scream when he let himself into the room. Or by a sultry hello, depending on which version of the redhead was the true one. Nonetheless, he checked the bathroom. It was empty. There was an electric razor, lady's version, lying on the edge of the bidet, its cord snaking to an outlet over the sink. The hunted frightened face in the mirror over the washbasin was his own. The smell of vomit and sweat lifted from him. The noise in the courtyard crescendoed, became frantic, and he stepped back into the room and walked toward the balcony, enveloping himself in the drapes. There was no mistaking the message the excited voices had brought back to Nerone. Giuseppe had been assassinated. Strangled. His clothing was disheveled. Perhaps he had been sexually assaulted.

"He is alone?" Puzzlement, almost fear, in Nerone's voice.

"He is lying on the floor, next to his bed, a wire around his neck. God in heaven, the expression in his eyes." Dancey could imagine the messenger's own eyes, round in horror.

"You saw no one else?"

A grim ghost of a smile formed on Dancey's lips. He had been right. Nerone expected them to find him in that room with Giuseppe. He had expected Dancey to be there. But Nerone? A priest? The prefect of the Vatican Library?

"The *carabinieri*," someone cried.

"Wait."

But Nerone's voice was lost in a chorus of demands for the police, the *carabinieri*. Some of the shouting voices grew fainter, as if executing the wishes of the others and going for official help. No doubt Nerone would soon be leading the constabulary in a charge on Dancey's room. How much time had he gained by breaking in next door?

He freed himself from the drapes, spinning to do so. His nausea returned and he stumbled toward the bathroom. He was going to be sick again.

12

Two circuits of the redhead's room convinced Dancey that there was only one way out and that not very promising. If he could have thought of another even half as promising, he would have taken it, but short of making a doomed dash through the lobby to the Via della Conciliazione or an equally doomed effort to get out the back way to the Borgo Santo Spirito, there was no other way.

He went into the bathroom, picked up an electric razor and set it awhir. With some reluctance he brought it to his beard; the beard was a symbol of something, though not of his manhood. Perhaps it was his badge of failure, a sign of his enlistment with the down and outs. But beards had become domesticated and respectable. Brokers and designers and construction workers wore beards. Professors wore beards. His was long overdue to come off, he decided, and he brought the gnatlike buzz of the razor into half a dozen years' growth. It snarled, it caught, it pulled, it made some progress of a patchy sort. Once he got the main growth down, he could concentrate on smoothness. The first stage was like preparing stone for the more careful chiseling to come. His skin, which he had expected to be deathly pale had somehow tanned along with the exposed parts of his face, though not of course to the same degree. At the moment, tan or no tan, he was a pale and shaken young man. It took him well over fifteen minutes before a clean-shaven version of himself looked back from the mirror. He stepped out of his trousers and began to shave his legs.

The agitated buzz of the razor seemed to carry with it excited exchanges from the courtyard below, and several times he turned it off and was surprised that nothing seemed to be going on out there. Just so, in a shower, one sometimes imagines conversations, ringing phones, a dozen things that are not there when the water is turned off. The thought suggested a bath, but he settled for a sponge bath when he had stripped down to his shorts, making use of the washbasin and, O harbinger, the bidet as well. He began to feel better until, thinking of what he was about to do, he felt bad again.

Transvestism was an aberration he had never understood. Perhaps that is the nature of an aberration, to be unintelligible to those unafflicted by it, but he had always been able to discover some semblance of sympathy, some tremor, however inchoate, of temptation, in reflecting on the other items in the Krafft-Ebing canon. But not this. Perhaps it was his very reluctance that made it possible for him to begin sorting through the redhead's clothes in search of an outfit to exit in. Among the dresses, there were slacks and a jacket of mannish cut. Odd. But the first item of business was the wig. It had been the sight of the wig case that had decided him on his mode of escape. The case contained two wigs, both red, and he wondered at the authenticity of the woman's hair color. Was she perhaps bald and in need of a *parrucca*? Her wigs had been bought in Rome, a city where wigmakers and wig shops flourished as nowhere else in Dancey's experience.

There was a mirror on the inside of the armoire door he had opened. He pulled the wig on, a tight fit, and then turned toward the mirror. His face registered his surprise at the transformation and then a smile crept over the countenance of the somewhat roguish wench who looked out at him. For the first time he had confidence in his plan. His own mother would not have recognized him in that wig. Now for shoes.

She had a dozen pairs, but a single glance at them filled Dancey with despair. He would never be able to get his foot into a shoe that small. Nonetheless he tried. He had been right the first time though. He managed to get four of his toes started into a shoe, but then his foot widened, and even if it hadn't he could not walk around flourishing his little toe like that. He was defeated. He sank back on the bed, caught a glimpse of himself in the mirror and bounded up again. The hair disguised him so perfectly that he could not give up. He would walk out barefoot if it came to that, carrying a pair of shoes in his hand and a plausible excuse for doing so on the tip of his tongue. A cab to a shoestore, the purchase of a pair that fit. His mind raced, but he seemed to be rejecting the thoughts even as they occurred. No. He had to be as inconspicuous as possible in leaving the hotel. Of course he would feel that the eyes of the world were upon him. Did he really prefer arrest as a female impersonator to whatever else he might be accused of? He did. Because that "whatever else" no doubt included both the murder of Giuseppe and the theft of the priceless Thomistic autograph from the Vatican Library.

And then he found the sandals. They consisted of a leather sole and a thong-like arrangement through which the big toe was pushed, and that was all. He tried them on. Though his heel hung over the heel of the sandal, that seemed a purist's quibble. He walked around the room, getting the hang of them. The trick was to slide the foot rather than lift it. This did things to his hips which in ordinary circumstances he would have found objectionable, but just then it seemed all to the good. He could have shouted with relief. The main difficulties, head and toe, had been resolved. The rest would be easy.

Well, easier. The problem was to find a dress that was not cut to display the considerable mammarian endowments of the redhead. Clearly she considered them her principal asset, since dress after dress plunged. The further issue suggested by this, one he had hoped to avoid, was that of underclothing. He opened a drawer and began to pull out panties and slips and bras. Padded bras! The vixen. How doubly dissembling of her to wear a padded bra and then a neckline that drew attention to her putative wares. Thank God for her vanity. But it is no easy matter, he then discovered, to don a brassiere. By putting the straps over his shoulders, he ended up with cups in his armpits, and when he clapped the cups to his chest, there seemed no way to get his arms through the straps without breaking them. He solved the problem by stepping into the bra, hoisting it and leaving the straps hang. If he survived the present danger, he would, he vowed, watch carefully the next time he was in the presence of a woman putting on a bra. Never mind that the next time would be the first time. But how would he explain the intensity of his interest?

He selected a flowery dress, pulled it over his head, zipped up the side and *eccola!* A woman. He stared at his mirrored image in disbelief. It was a bit shattering to realize that a fairly passable woman could be made of even such poor material as he offered. Had he been perhaps too easily satisfied in the past? He stepped back, turned, postured, observed himself with his chin hung over his shoulder. He played the coquette, batting his lashes. He wiggled his ass and shook his phony tits at the mirror. Does she or doesn't she?

All dressed up and someplace, anyplace, to go, he now began to think of reasons to postpone his departure. It was going on six o'clock. Good God, his watch. He couldn't wear that. And he would need a purse. He found something better, a shoulder bag that was jammed with female paraphernalia. He dumped its contents onto the bed and filled it with his discarded clothing. The cosmetics on the bed made him wonder about make-up. He found a lipstick and went into the bathroom.

Leaning toward the mirror, he stretched his lips and brought the tube toward them. He stopped. Clothes were one thing, more or less external, but to put on lipstick would carry him across a line he had so far been only skirting. Just then he heard voices in the hallway, real and not imaginary voices, and he began to apply lipstick lavishly to his mouth. Afterwards he worked his lips the way women do, and the result—he felt constrained to admit it—was devastating. He actually felt like a woman now, psychological-ly, inside. The whole thing seemed less an act and his confidence fairly inflated until there came a knock on the door. Hardly breathing, he stepped into the room. The knocking came again, impatient.

"Yes?" Far too exaggerated, his tone sounded like that of a dowager in a comedy.

"Mrs. Parson?" It was the head honcho from the desk. "Are you there, Mrs. Parson?"

Was he Mrs. Parson? "What is it?"

"Would you open the door, please?"

His debut could not be postponed. He stepped to the door, wet his lips, turned the knob and pulled the door open with a grand gesture. With an instinct that surprised him, he leaned forward, leading with his padded bra, and looked at the chief clerk through his lashes. Overacting, overacting, a voice within him cried, but his audience did not seem to think so. The clerk was flanked by two policemen in the dark blue uniform of the *carabinieri*.

"You are alone, signorina?" one of them asked.

"Signora," he corrected coyly. "Is something the matter?" He put a hand to his throat, then wished he hadn't. He had neglected to shave the backs of his hands. He swiftly transferred his hand to the clerk's sleeve. "Tell me, please. What is wrong?"

"Nothing is wrong," the clerk cried, assuming a phony smile. "A routine check, madame. Please excuse us."

"But you can tell me. I am brave."

"No, no, madame. There is no need for bravery. Everything is all right."

One of the *carabinieri* seemed to be watching Dancey more closely than the other, and he wondered if he had been wise to prolong the exchange at the door. Suddenly the figure of Roberto Nerone appeared behind the three in his doorway. Nerone was in street clothes and did not seem to be wearing a Roman collar. Dancey was certain he would be recognized, but Nerone's eyes hardly grazed him. "There are other rooms," he said coldly.

After Dancey had shut the door, his first impulse was to laugh triumphantly, but then the weakness in his knees suggested that hubris was to be avoided. And so was delay. He must move now, when his presence was expected, when Mrs. Parson was known to be in the hotel. He shouldered the bag he had packed with his own clothes, opened the hall door once more and stepped outside. The clerk and the *carabinieri* were speaking with another guest, several doors away. Nerone was nowhere in sight. Dancey decided to go down the front way, through the lobby.

Two minutes later he was on the street. To his left the dome of St. Peter's shone in the setting sun. He turned to the right and came face to face with Mrs. Parson. She had just got out of a cab and turned to enter the hotel. Her eyes went rapidly over Dancey and seemed to come to rest at his hair. It was identical to her own. Her mouth opened and she seemed about to speak, but Dancey brushed past her and climbed into the cab.

"The airport," he cried, and pulled the door closed.

The driver wheeled away from the curb and into traffic before he looked back. "Is something wrong, signora?" He seemed dumbstruck to see Dancey there. "Did you say the airport?"

"What do you mean, wrong?"

"But I just left you . . . "

Ah. He actually thought Dancey was Mrs. Parson. Perfect. The driver had already launched into a discussion of the fare to the airport, licking his chops as he did so.

"I don't want to go to the airport. Take me to the place where you picked me up."

"The Columbus Hotel?" His face fell.

"No, no, no. Are you stupid? Take me to where you picked me up before you drove me to the hotel."

"You want to go back there?"

"Yes," Dancey said firmly, and settled back in the seat.

He wondered where the driver had picked her up. It was necessary to assume that his manner was explained by disappointment at not getting the airport bonanza. Dancey's plan, insofar as he had a plan, was to sow confusion. Mrs. Parson would claim to have seen herself getting back into the cab. The driver would say that it had indeed been Mrs. Parson who reentered his cab and asked to be returned to her point of departure. Time would be wasted on all this. Time would be gained by Dancey. Time for what? He needed time even to figure out what he needed time for. When he had shouted the airport as his destination, he had been trying instinctively to mislead Mrs. Parson, who would not, he was sure, soon forget the woman with hair just like her own and wearing a dress that was the spitting image of one in her own armoire. But there had also been the mad fleeting hope that he might dash to the airport and board the first plane out of Italy. Of course that would have entailed showing his passport, and in his present getup, no customs man in the world would have let him through. Security at Fiumicino was frenetic if ineffective, with dozens of cops wearing crushed caps sauntering about with pistols at their belts and doubtless others in plain clothes, now that irrational violence might materialize at any airport in the West.

The driver had taken the Lungotevere, following the river, and Dancey tried to relax, tried to appear the somewhat flaky foreigner he must seem, changing her mind and retracing a route she had just taken. The man was talking to himself in a not fully audible way, commenting on the traffic and, Dancey was sure, his puzzling passenger. His radio crackled with messages and, as if reminded, he picked up his microphone.

"Number 733 on my way to the Great Synagogue."

The synagogue! Good grief. But then Dancey thought of the narrow streets of the Roman ghetto. Perfect. He could get lost in the crowd there until he decided what he must do next. The driver crossed the river and minutes later pulled to the curb on the side of the street nearest the river and called out the fare.

The fare. Money. My God. His money was in his trousers, which were stuffed in the bag he carried. He unzipped it and began to dig around. The smell of dry vomit filled the cab and the driver turned frowning to him and repeated that he was owed four hundred lire. Dancey had found his pocket and his wallet and he pulled it out, revealing the filthy leg of his trousers as he did so. Thrusting a five-hundred-lire note into the driver's hand, he opened the door and jumped out, the trouser leg fluttering from the bag. He stuffed it inside and zipped up the bag. The driver did not pull away.

Crossing the street, weaving among the careening cars, the object of irate horns and one or two obscene suggestions, he got to the opposite curb. The driver, when he looked back, was staring after his passenger. There seemed little else for Dancey to do but enter the synagogue. He went up the stairs and pulled open the heavy door and stepped inside.

Cool, dark, from far off the ululation of prayer. He had never been in a synagogue before and he had no idea what one might do there at this time of evening. Or at any other time, for that matter. The fact that he was dressed as a woman seemed to complicate things. He had a vague notion that women were not much seen in synagogues. The street door opened and an old man came in. His jeweler's eye bore into Dancey but he said nothing. Perhaps he sensed that Dancey was on the run and that made him Jew enough for him. He shuffled on into the main part of the synagogue. Dancey held the street door before it closed completely, and peered out. The cab was still there.

It was still there a minute later when he looked again. The driver had his microphone in his hand and there was little doubt possible that he was keeping an eye on the door of the synagogue. It was the microphone that decided Dancey. The driver was in contact with his dispatcher, who could be in contact with the police. Perhaps Mrs. Parson had sounded the alarm as soon as she entered the hotel and the driver had been contacted by his dispatcher. Dancey slapped down the steps, hurried up the sidewalk and then plunged into a narrow street that led away from the river. The smell of fish and of non-Italian cooking assailed him; there were kids playing in the streets, clothes hanging from lines strung between buildings over the narrow passageways. The sun had all but set. Of course it had been dark in these streets for an hour already. He came to a small square with a fountain in the form of a turtle. He had to get to a phone. If the adversary could communicate, so could he. He saw the little blue sign of a tobacco store and headed for it. A bell tinkled when he came through the door.

"Un gettone, per favore," he said to the woman behind the

counter. He had kept his wallet convenient after the scare in the cab. The woman looked at him with mild surprise. Her surprise turned to irritation when he handed her a bill. The smallest note he had was ten thousand lire. She asked him if he had anything else. The telephone token cost only fifteen lire—seven cents and dropping.

"Give me some cigarettes," Dancey said. "Ten packages."

"Ten!"

"Yes. Ten." He pushed the ten-thousand-lire note at her. He would gladly pay that much to use the phone. She had stacked ten packages of Nazionali cigarettes on the counter with an alacrity that impressed. This was a sale she wanted to make before he could change his mind. The woman plunked down a *gettone* for the phone. Dancey would not soon be forgotten here, he thought with dismay. What a trail he was leaving for his pursuers. And he had no doubt now that they were in pursuit of him. The body of Giuseppe would be a powerful stimulus.

"Do you have a directory?"

She indicated where it was, next to the telephone. Dancey glided across to it, the thongs of the sandals rubbing painfully between his toes. With the huge Rome directory open before him like a Domesday Book, he looked up Bertello, Polly. There were many Bertellos. There was no Polly Bertello. There was no Bertello who lived at an address he could identify as close to the Piazza del Popolo. The woman behind the counter was watching him, openly amused.

"Your cigarettes," she said, indicating the pile before her. Dancey's change lay next to this record sale.

He crossed to her, put the cigarettes into his bag, trying to open it only enough to cram them in, but her beady eye seemed to inspect the strange contents. And again the odor of vomit was in the air. The woman's brows drew closer together. Dancey put the change into the bag after the cigarettes. The *gettone* was still in his hand.

"Can't you remember the number?"

"I've forgotten the address."

"Perhaps I can help." He seemed to be providing her with a

welcome diversion. What might this woman do next?

"Thank you. It will come to me if I don't think of it."

She approved this logic of reminiscence. Dancey left the store, the little bell rang and, at the same time, the woman shouted a man's name, her tone fruity with amusement. Paolo would not believe the woman who had just been in. *Pazza.* Loony. Ten packages of cigarettes and she uses her purse for a laundry bag.

The sandals would have been hard on his feet even if they had fit. As it was, with the thong strangling his big toe and his overhanging heel taking punishment from the cobbles, he found it difficult to hurry. He continued to move in a direction away from the river, not following any one street more than from one intersection to the next, making a leisurely zigzag, now north, now south. He passed several telephones but did not stop. There was no point in it since he did not have Polly's number. Had there even been a phone in her apartment? To ask the question was to invite doubt. On the one hand, he had a vivid image of it sitting on the floor, next to a rattan chair; on the other, it seemed so obviously a product of his need for help that he was sure he imagined it. But of course she had a phone. He had called her the day before, before their picnic at the beach. Real or imaginary, though, her phone was of no help to him without its number.

He looked down the street he was now on and saw a police car slide past the intersection; his heart rose in his throat. And then it appeared again, backing up. Had they seen him and recognized their prey? Without hesitation, he stepped into a doorway. He came into a small hall that seemed out of harmony with the street outside and the exterior of the building. Terracotta pieces were embedded in the walls and there was a rectangular brass insert—mailboxes. The building contained apartments, and obviously not those of the poor. A wrought-iron railing followed the stairs out of sight above and he mounted them, slipping off the sandals to make better progress. He reached a landing; there were two doors, each with a nameplate. The stairs continued up and so did he. Removing the sandals suggested the obvious course. Between floors, he pulled off the wig and unzipped the dress and stepped out of it. He stood there, bare to the waist, except for that absurd bra, when he heard the street door open and then feet on the stairs. He snatched up his bag and hurried higher on the stairs and he knew the sensation of hair rising from his scalp. Insane explanations were forming in his mind when he realized that the footsteps were no longer ascending. There was the sound of nervous whistling, a key in a lock, a door opening. When it shut, he sank on the stone steps, his breathing short, shallow, rapid. Was it possible to have a heart attack at age twenty-six? But this was a day when nothing in the nature of disaster seemed impossible.

He got out of the bra by sliding it down over his hips and then stepping free of it. The clothes he pulled from the bag were smelly and crumpled. It was a relief to put on his trousers nonetheless. He placed his shirt on the step beside him and put the wig and dress and bra and sandals into the bag. When it was zipped up, he felt that he had assumed a new disguise, that of a beardless boy. On with his wrinkled shirt then. Suddenly he felt lighter, renewed, capable of anything. He started down the stairs and they were cold on his bare feet. His bare feet! He backed up the stairs, unzipped the bag and groped inside it. But he had apparently forgotten to pack his own shoes. Groaning, he got out the sandals and put them on. He was considerably less buoyant when he started down the stairs again.

On the first landing, he wondered which door it was that had opened a minute before when his hair was standing on end and his heart was palpitating like a cornered animal's. On the street floor he noticed a door opposite that through which he had entered and he went to it. It gave onto the inevitable courtyard. It was a lovely hidden thing with gravel walks, flowerbeds, a nude statue greening on a plinth in the center. On three sides it was contained by the high walls of buildings, but the fourth was a fence of brick, ten feet high, concealing what? His head, though released from the wig, began unaccountably to sweat. He wiped at his brow and was reminded of the bandage hooding the fingertip that Lancia had pricked. He felt like a wounded animal being pursued through territory he did not know. The vast unfairness of what had befallen him filled him with a desire to cry out in anguish. The sight of a wooden door in the wall enabled him to stifle his rage.

His feet made an odd sound on the gravel as he walked through the garden, praying that the door in the wall would not be locked. There was no lock. There was no handle either. Just the featureless expanse of the door. It looked as if it had never been opened. Dancey pushed against it and it gave out a small complaint. He shifted the bag that he had slung over his shoulder, and looking back, he saw a couple seated on a balcony peer down at him with wary interest. From a distance came the distinctive wail of a siren, rising, falling, an eerie, unearthly sound at any time, but at that moment productive of panic.

He turned and pushed at the gate, hard, and it opened, not wide, perhaps a foot. There seemed to be something on the far side preventing it from opening further. He gave another mighty shove and stepped through the opening, curling his big toe in order to keep a grip on the sandal. There was a clatter on the other side, but there was no going back now. When he had squeezed through the reluctant opening he found himself in an alleyway. He had tipped over a trash can and a huge cat, back raised, hissed at him. He hissed back. Events seemed to have returned him to the antic, unreasonable reactions of childhood. The hissing was like a safety valve.

The building backing the alley had an open door and Dancey could see right through to a street. He scooted along the passage, aware of pungent odors and the sound of many voices, as if a dozen family arguments were going on at once. Before stepping out into the street, he stood and looked from left to right. Across the street, at an angle, a very fat woman loomed over a man seated on a doorstep. No one else. But still he looked left and right, left and right, as if in search of a tennis match. Nothing. He hitched the bag higher on his shoulder, stepped into the street and began to walk as fast as he could while still appearing nonchalant. He took the direction away from the river, which he associated with the perfidious driver, but of course danger was not confined to that direction. The police car, perhaps many, would be moving among these narrow streets. But they were looking for a redheaded woman and Dancey was now a disheveled young man going home for the night, from work, from shopping, from a glass of wine.

The street led him, as any street in Rome eventually does, to a piazza. He loitered at the mouth of the street and looked out over the great expanse. There were stalls everywhere and hundreds of people, and the jabber of their voices was like a heavenly choir. A market. And there, looming above the stalls and milling people, was the brooding hulk of Giordano Bruno. This was the Campo dei Fiori! Oriented, delighted with the crowd and the anonymity it promised, Dancey entered the piazza and began to stroll among the shoppers. The wares in the stalls had been picked over all day and looked it. Tomatoes, zucchini, onions, meat—great slabs of it lying on counters under clouds of flies—fish, chickens. Plucked, pale, skinny, these hung as though in a mass execution. The dozens of conflicting smells made Dancey dizzy, but he felt safe. The haggling, the elbowing, the color and chatter, and the somber visage of Bruno disapproving of it all, reassured him as nothing else could have. Yet he could not feel anonymous. People glanced at him strangely, often with disgust. His beardless face? His shoulder bag? His clothes? He did not know. All he knew was that there was no safety here where there should have been. He should have been able to lose himself in this throng and wander about until he knew exactly what he would do next. Halfway through the piazza he turned and looked up a narrow street and saw the tricolor fluttering from an upper window of the Farnese Palace. The French Embassy!

The American Embassy! It was located on the Via Veneto, which, he realized with a sinking feeling, was a long way from where he then was, but it was so obviously the place to go that he shouldered his way through a knot of shoppers and headed rapidly toward the far corner of the piazza.

He would not take main streets. He would continue to favor small, narrow, out-of-the-way streets. This decision was prompted by the odd interest he had raised in the shoppers of the Campo dei

Fiori. If he could not be inconspicuous in crowds, crowds were no advantage. Better then the obscurity of dark side streets.

The American Embassy. He could remember it vividly, and the consulate next door, imposing structures on the Via Veneto as one came up past the Capuchin church with its grottoes constructed of bones of the monks of yesteryear. That grisly memory was also vivid, though it was more than a decade old. He had had nightmares after going there, and his mother had scolded his father for taking him. The thought of his father, in his present plight, was an invitation to grieve. He felt as if the loss were a recent one rather than an absence with which he had lived for nearly half his conscious life. He realized that he had been praying as he fled and now it seemed that he had been addressing his dead father too. He would protect Jimmy. He would see that he got to the embassy safely. If the souls of the departed haunt particular places, it seemed to Dancey that his father would certainly have chosen Rome for his ghostly habitation.

The embassy was a surrogate father, he supposed, a place where his innocence would be unquestioned and protection extended automatically. All he had to do was go up to the door and . . . And what? Tell them that he had lost an invaluable manuscript while on an unauthorized mission for the Vatican Library, that he had fainted at the sight of his own blood during a physical examination, that he had woken up in bed with a dead porter and had fled his hotel dressed as a woman? Not even a father could accept that tale without blanching. The main thing was that he had not killed Giuseppe. He was prepared to take the blame for the loss of the manuscript, but it must be clearly understood that he had had no part in the death of Giuseppe. The murder of Giuseppe. They would believe him at the embassy, he assured himself, and of course it was a species of whistling in the dark. Nonetheless he preferred reciting his incredible story to his countrymen rather than to the Italian police.

The difficulty with taking side streets is that the streets of Rome resist parallels more certainly than does non-Euclidean geometry. When he crossed Vittorio Emanuele and avoided entering the

Piazza Navona, Dancey had taken a street that promised to lead him to the Corso. So he was taken aback when he suddenly emerged at the river. Trying desperately to get his bearings, he began to follow the river road. He was further astounded when, in the gathering twilight, the Castel Sant' Angelo and, beyond it, the dome of St. Peter's suddenly loomed before him. Had he been doubling back on himself? He knew that the Tiber takes a serpentine course through Rome and it was equally clear to him that side streets make for crooked progress, but just where the hell was he?

His sense of familiarity with Rome depended greatly on keeping in contact with landmarks, yet there was St. Peter's and he had no idea at all where he was. Even if he had somehow doubled back to the river he had thought he was leaving, he felt no temptation now to retrace his steps to some point where he could correct his error. For one in flight, to go deliberately back is to seek out his pursuers. So he continued along the river road, walking neither fast nor slow, hoping that soon he would see something that would give him a clue as to where he was.

Walking without any sure sense of direction is an unnerving experience, particularly when pursuers may pop around any corner. Dancey pushed ahead, resenting his progress, yet anxious to keep on the move. And then, just like that, he knew where he was. The Piazza del Popolo! Of course. And the Piazza del Popolo meant Polly. It no longer mattered that he did not have her telephone number. He would pay a call in person.

The *portiera*, when Dancey found the place, stared at him suspiciously, and he could hardly blame her, given the way he must have looked, but he was in no mood to be patient with officious menials. She in turn was reluctant to admit that anyone remotely like Polly even lived in the building, so how could she ring her up on the intercom?

"She has a studio on the top floor," Dancey said, handing the crone a thousand-lire note. "Signorina Bertello. I'll just go up."

"You can't do that. I must ring first."

"Then ring."

She opened her hand to check the denomination of the bill he had slipped her. "*Momento.*" But Polly did not answer the ring.

"That's all right," Dancey said. "She's expecting me."

And with that, he stepped into the elevator. The crone rose from her chair, bleating, protesting, but he had punched the top button on the console and the door slid closed. He hoped that a thousand lire would placate her until Polly returned. She could consider her duty done if she warned Polly that someone awaited her upstairs.

The key was where Polly had taken it from last night. Last night. It seemed a week ago that he had shared her bed. The thought of that bed overwhelmed him and it was all he could do to get the door shut behind him, having returned the key to its hiding place in a flowerpot in the hall. The cat came and nuzzled his ankles, then began to sniff in earnest. He shooed it away from his caked and odorous trousers. The bed was unmade. Good enough. He fell upon it as if it were an infinitely desirable mistress. He hugged to himself a pillow that still carried traces of Polly, and feeling at last safe and snug, he slipped smiling into sleep. He had outwitted them all.

Sometime during the night he felt her undoing his belt and tugging off his trousers. Then she was beside him, pulling the covers over them, adapting her body to his, putting her arms around him. The womb must have been something like that.

It was not yet quite light when he awoke. Polly had rolled away from him as she slept and her hands were crossed chastely over her breast. It was the only part of her that was covered. She made an interesting sight and one which, his strength renewed by sleep, he found it hard only to contemplate. Yet it seemed unfair to waken her so early. How early? His cheap new watch was in the bag he had pitched onto the rattan chair before he collapsed on the bed. It was only necessary to wait and listen for church bells. As Polly had observed, they were surrounded by churches. He seemed to have waited over fifteen minutes before a bell sounded. Once. And then there were other bells, each ringing uninformatively once. The quarter-hour. Perhaps it had been the ringing of the hour that had wakened him. He turned to Polly, to find that she was looking at him. Her sleepy eyes squinted in a smile.

"Hello," he said.

"Your lipstick is smeared."

13

Not as much as it was shortly thereafter. Polly, driven perhaps by a smidgen of the perversity Dancey had felt in applying it, mashed his painted mouth with hers until he could taste lipstick as vividly as he had on a first date years before when all his dreams of abandoned necking had come true in the arms of a little blond Norwegian. He felt restored after his sleep, but not to the extent required by Polly's ardor. She might have been welcoming back someone given up for lost. With some anxiety, Dancey looked for signs of her flagging in the long minutes that followed her awakening. When she finally did release him, he felt discarded. Propped on her elbows, she looked down at him with a small off-center smile.

"You look funny without a beard."

"You don't."

"What on earth have you been up to?"

"You're not in the book."

"The telephone directory? Sure I am."

"There is no Polly Bertello in the Rome directory."

"I didn't say there was." Her eyes went to the wall, then came back. "I use my married name. Osborne."

Even if that had occurred to him the night before, it would not have helped, but the fact was that he had not thought of it. Of course Polly would use her maiden name in identifying herself to someone she had known before her marriage.

"I tried to call," he said.

"Oh, Jimmy." She laid a hand on his arm, canted her head and looked at him as only a mother should. "Running through the streets like that. Tell me about the lipstick and all the lovely clothes in your shoulder bag." Her elbow nudged his ribs. "How long have you been skulking around in drag?"

"Polly, I'm in trouble. Real trouble."

"You should see the cases we've cured." She stretched for and got the wig. She put it on. The transformation excited Dancey and he reached for her. He changed his mind, not wanting to activate her again.

He said, "You ought to wear a wig."

"I am. What kind of trouble?" She pulled the wig from her head and sailed it toward Mrs. Parson's shoulder bag. "Tell me."

All he had to do was begin at the beginning, but it was hard to know where that was, exactly, so he began at the end. Or was it the middle? Giuseppe dead. The manuscript gone. And then he had to explain who Giuseppe was. Polly's face provided a running commentary on the credibility of his tale. Her expression was receptive as he began, but a frown formed when he described waking up beside the dead Giuseppe.

"Who gave you the beer that you think . . . "

"That did. Yes."

"And his room is down the hall from yours?"

No. It was down a flight of stairs and he did not know how he had got there. But enough of Giuseppe, God rest his soul; the little porter had pocketed his last tip. The Thomistic manuscript was gone.

"I've let them all down, Polly. They trusted me with something that is absolutely irreplaceable. That manuscript is so priceless that . . . well . . . " He could see the parchment, see the unintelligible handwriting of the saint. It was a crime to be carting that around the streets as if it were the one millionth copy of a paperback thriller.

"Maybe they retrieved it, Jimmy. Maybe it isn't lost."

His heart leaped with hope, but then he remembered Nerone in the courtyard. If Nerone did not know where the manuscript was—and why otherwise had he taken part in the search of the hotel?—then it had not been retrieved. It had been stolen.

"But who?"

"Polly, there are people who would give . . ." But he could think of no adequate collateral. "Lots of people would want it. It is unique."

"How many knew about it?"

That was a good question. He told her so. It was *the* question. Others knew about the manuscript. And they had drugged him, killed Giuseppe . . .

"Jimmy, they might have killed you!"

"The thought crossed my mind." Her knuckles in his ribs. "That is why the lipstick and the goddam women's clothes. I had to get out of there before they emasculated me."

She put her arms around him and began to rock him gently. This was the haven he had hungered for during his terrified flight. No need to mention that it had been Nerone in the courtyard, Nerone in the corridor, Nerone as pursuer, who had decided him on flight. He had been frightened, yes. But what he had been running from, more than anything else, was the realization that he had betrayed those who had trusted him. "You are perfect for our purposes." Nerone's words in the Café di Napoli. They had etched themselves into Dancey's mind. As if into stone, he thought ruefully. A monumental error. How could he blame Nerone for being enraged?

Polly continued to rock him and eventually sleep returned, but sleep was no refuge from his anxieties. Restlessly tossing, he fled in dreams through narrow streets, bewigged, improperly shod, demanding of shadowy passers-by directions to the Great Synagogue of Rome.

When he awoke, Polly was already up. Apparently she had been up for some time. She had rinsed out his clothes and draped them like a naval message over the ledge of the balcony. Their message was clear enough to Dancey: Giuseppe dead, a priceless manuscript entrusted to Dancey's care stolen.

"Stay in bed," Polly urged. "You can have breakfast there."

Her smile was gay and conspiratorial. Sun streamed in from the balcony. The apartment seemed a metaphor of peace, of untroubled life, of Rome as he had remembered it. Thus of a morning had the sun shone into their apartment on Mount Parioli. He felt his throat constrict. Polly, in a bright summer dress as yellow as the morning, full-skirted, twirled around the room, busy as could be. How vulnerable she looked.

"I'd like to see the papers."

"Of course," she cried. "I'll get them. I'll get some rolls too. Water's hot for tea."

She threw him a kiss and was gone. He sprang from bed as soon as the door shut behind her. He dashed onto the balcony and began pulling his damp clothes from the line. He had to get out of this apartment. From the time he landed in Rome, disaster had been with him. A massacre at the airport and now this, a manuscript lost, a porter dead. Giuseppe. Use the man's name. Give him that at least. Would his death make the morning paper? Would the loss of the manuscript?

Pulling on his wet clothes was like reoccupying the terror of the night before. He had brought danger with him to Polly's apartment and that was unforgivable. Last night, okay, he had been so scared and tired he had not been thinking straight. Now in the light of morning he knew that he could not do this to her. He would leave and take disaster with him.

He was going to find out what had happened to that manuscript. He had thought of the way to begin.

14

Once outside the apartment, he started toward the Stazione Termini, at first fearful that he would be seen by Polly. As that fear receded, another took its place: fear of a pursuer whose face he did not know. He kept to the sunny side of the street, but it would take hours before these cold, clammy clothes would dry. They were the least of his worries, no matter that sleepy citizens gave him startled glances. He must have looked like Lazarus emerging in his grave clothes.

The muscles of his legs protested this renewal of flight. The wet trousers flapping against his calves threatened cramps. Would he crumple to the sidewalk, drowning in air, undone at last? He scoffed at the thought. Inadequate as his sleep had been, he was glad to be out and about. A new emotion pressed at the edges of his confusion, anger driving out remorse. What a fool he had been!

He had his choice of phone booths when he arrived at the Stazione Termini, and he took the one that seemed most exposed to the sun. It would be possible to sit in it until his clothes were dry. Mother Nature's laundry. But first things first. Getting seated in the booth, he eased his fiery feet from the sandals and looked up Strommer's number. Using the *gettone* he had bought from the woman in the ghetto, he dialed it.

"*Pronto.*"

"Signor Strommer, *per favore.*"

"Who is speaking, please?"

The sound of traffic made it difficult to hear, but Strommer's caution encouraged Dancey. Ulrich Strommer sounded like a man for whom things were going very badly indeed. Did that put them in the same boat?

"Dancey."

"What! Who is this?" Strommer's voice was strangled with emotion. Panic? Fear? For all Dancey could tell, it might be joy.

"It's me. James Dancey."

There was a long pause during which Dancey was afraid Strommer would hang up and cut off the sound of his heavy breathing. But he did not. When he spoke again, it was in an oddly modulated tone.

"Is that you, Gainer?"

"Goddam it, Strommer. This is Dancey. I have to talk to you. Something terrible has happened."

"Continue to speak."

"What the hell do you mean?"

"Is it really you, Dancey?"

"Strommer, something has happened to the manuscript. To the Thomistic autograph. I can't bring it back. I don't have it." Again he was assailed by the memory of that parchment. He remembered the awe with which Strommer had shown him what he would be taking out of the Vatican.

"You stole it," Strommer said with a meditative groan. "You stole it, Dr. Dancey. We trusted you. We all trusted you, and you betrayed us." His heavy breathing accelerated. "Poor Père Jacques."

"I have to talk to you. Then you can explain to Jacques that I did not betray you."

"Jacques is in the hospital."

"Oh, no!"

"Oh yes, Dancey. He had a stroke when he learned that you had stolen the manuscript."

"Dear God!" He did not dare dwell on thoughts of that frail little priest, whispering among his treasured manuscripts, worrying about their safety and vetoing any further effort to make a filmed record of them. Who would have dreamed that things could go as

112

wrong as they had? But Dancey did not care for the way Strommer was putting the blame entirely on him. "I did not steal that manuscript, Strommer."

"I have no money, Dancey. I cannot pay you for it."

"I haven't got it! Strommer, I was knocked out. I might have been killed. Giuseppe was killed. The manuscript was stolen."

"Why are you calling me?" And then, in an altered tone, "Where are you now?"

"I have to see you."

"Very well." Strommer spoke with infinite resignation. "Come to my apartment."

"Wouldn't that be dangerous?"

"I don't understand."

"A man has been killed, Strommer. How is Monsignor Nerone taking all this?"

"Do you have my address?"

Dancey read the address from the telephone directory. "Is that right?"

"You're coming here?"

"I have to talk to you. I have to talk to someone. What the hell happened? What went wrong? I don't know."

Strommer fell silent and Dancey was embarrassed by his own outburst. Strommer asked, "When will you get here?"

"I don't know. Give me an hour." Actually he should have been able to get there by bus in fifteen minutes, but he had lost faith in timetables and their spurious precision.

"Very well."

After Dancey had hung up by depressing the bar, he sat on with the phone pressed to his ear. Strommer had reacted to his call with disbelief. Why? Had he been surprised at being contacted by the putative thief? Or had he thought Dancey was dead? That could have been the plan. Implicate the stupid American and then get rid of him.

Next to the modern structure of the train terminal, there was a fragment of one of the ancient walls that had been built to protect the city. It had been left where it was, a relic of the past allowed to survive in a modern setting. Looking at it through the streaked dirty glass of the phone booth, Dancey felt nostalgic for a time when safety could be found in walls and fortifications, in preparations against a palpable enemy who would arrive on foot, take up space, require a common ground on which to move. By contrast, he felt threatened by unknown dangers that might arrive from anywhere without notice.

Dancey left the booth and found his bus, and seated by a window, he stared unseeing out of it. Whether or not he had thought Dancey dead, what was Strommer's source of information about what had happened at the Columbus Hotel? It was becoming difficult to think of the fat German scholar as, like himself, an innocent victim of the microfiche project gone awry.

Dancey dismounted from the bus at the Piazza Bologna and walked back toward the street off the Via Nomentana on which Strommer lived. The bus had passed it before he spotted the sign and would not have stopped there in any case. The piazza was redolent of diesel fuel exhaust and coffee, of flowers and fruit. Dancey felt faint with hunger in this busy place which did not seem nearly busy enough. His wet and wrinkled clothes made him dangerously conspicuous. He could not convince himself that his fear was irrational. No one would be looking for him in this part of Rome.

A policeman's helmet loomed ahead and Dancey turned immediately and walked the opposite way. At a traffic light, he crossed with the crowd, then he cut across the garden in the center of the piazza and got the hell out of there. The street he left the piazza on was not the Nomentana. After walking a block, he cut to the left at the newspaper offices of the MSI, a right-wing party, where huge headlines warned of dire electoral results, got to the Viale XXI Aprile and continued west.

The revolving light was the first thing he saw when he turned the corner into Strommer's street. Cars were stopped every which way in the street and people were emerging from the doors of buildings, to add to the gathering crowd. The revolving light was on top of a police ambulance. Dancey approached the scene like a sleepwalker, moving among the stopped cars, joining the crowd. Without explicitly forming the thought, he had already guessed what had happened. The only question was how. Over the heads of the people he could not jostle aside, he saw the object on the street. A blanket had been thrown over it, but the shape of a human body was unmistakable. A fat, familiar human body.

"Did a car hit him?" he asked a woman standing beside him. She was hugging herself and her dirty fingernails dug into her bare upper arms.

"He jumped," she said, with awe in her voice. A bare arm lifted. "From his balcony." Her eyes bored into Dancey's, as if to transfer dread. "I *heard* him. Aaaaeeee." She imitated the sound, almost in a whisper, and her eyes enlarged with the horrible memory.

Dancey's eyes went back to the blanketed body on the pavement, which was indistinguishable from the body of Porres on the floor of the terminal at Fiumicino. Porres, Giuseppe, and now Strommer. He moved along the edge of the crowd. One pudgy hand protruded from the blanket. Strommer's hand, but it was no longer Strommer's hand. At that moment, a very live hand closed firmly around Dancey's arm and he turned to face Ernesto Cielli.

With a shake of the head, Cielli discouraged conversation. He tugged Dancey's sleeve, let it go, turned and walked away. Dancey followed, instinctively keeping at a slight distance: two men, their curiosity assuaged, returning to quotidian concerns. At the corner, Cielli stopped and waited for him.

"This is no place for you, Dancey. Where the hell have you been?"

How much did Cielli know? Dancey had no reason to believe that he knew anything.

"We've been looking for you all night," Cielli said. He started to walk and Dancey fell in beside him. "An American at the hotel called to tell us of the ruckus there."

"Giuseppe was killed. You met him. A porter."

A small smile flitted across Cielli's face. "One doesn't meet porters, Dancey. Did you kill him?"

"I'm lucky I wasn't killed myself."

Cielli grew solemn. "You may be right. We can have a cup of coffee in the Piazza Bologna. You get caught in the rain or something?"

"Or something. Cielli, the police are after me."

"My dear fellow, what have I been telling you? Not to worry. We will take care of you."

Dancey found these words infinitely reassuring. The American consulate to the rescue. They would not permit an innocent man to suffer. His raging hunger returned. He wanted a lot more than a cup of coffee.

15

"You are a wanted man," Cielli said, stirring a third packet of sugar into his coffee. On the way to the piazza, he had tried to persuade Dancey to come directly to the consulate. For dry clothes, if nothing else. They both knew that was not the reason. But Dancey, literally faint from hunger, had no stomach for caution now. Besides, with Cielli he felt safe, almost in protective custody. He was no longer just a bewildered man plunging alone through the streets of the city. "You like those doughnuts?"

Dancey nodded.

"Why are you wanted?" Cielli asked. "A man has been killed. A porter. For some reason, you are suspected of the crime, the scene of which you fled." He opened his hands. "These are all the facts we have."

"I didn't kill him."

"But why did you run? That was bound to draw attention. And you shaved off your beard."

"Cielli, I was scared." Not the whole truth, maybe, but true enough.

"I wish you had called the consulate, Dancey. That's what we're for. You have complicated our job by running away."

They were seated at a white metal café table under the trees in the piazza, the area enclosed by glass partitions, which were a barrier to whatever winds might blow as well as to the noise of traffic. Cielli's coffee cup looked miniature in his paw of a hand; his powerful body seemed wedged into the chair, yet at the same time he gave the impression of being on his mark. Dancey's fear was gone. Earlier he had hurried through this piazza, terrified by the sight of a policeman's helmet. His present sense of security made Strommer's death even more horrible to think about.

Ulrich Strommer is dead. A simple declarative sentence. Language is an awesome thing, capable of containing such uncontainable truths as that. Porres's body had lain on the floor of customs at the airport, covered, an object, dead. And now a man to whom Dancey had spoken within the hour had fallen from his balcony and lay dead in the street.

"Fallen?" Cielli said, his smile gone for good.

"Did anyone say he jumped?"

Cielli bowed his head. But either way was incredible. Dancey replayed in his mind what Strommer had said to him on the phone, trying to find some hint that the German had been thinking of throwing himself off his balcony. Strommer, who had thought Dancey was dead. Strommer, who had wondered if it was Gainer calling him, pretending to be Dancey. Strommer, who was abject at Jacques's reaction to the loss of the Thomistic manuscript. Only the last could have produced despair.

And yet, at the end of the telephone conversation, Strommer had spoken as if he was expecting Dancey. He had wondered how long it would be before he arrived. My God, had he been calculating how much time he had before Dancey got there, how much time to screw up his courage and take the fatal plunge? If that was the case—and Dancey found it hard to reject the idea once he had thought it—he had become an unwitting executioner. Again. His path through Rome was strewn with bodies.

Cielli said, "He was pushed."

"How did you know that?"

"It was the talk of the street, Dancey. You see why I was anxious to get you away from there. We do not want you connected with still another corpse. How long had you been there, by the way?"

Cielli lofted the question over Dancey's head, as if it were an idle query. But of course its implications could not be entirely concealed by asking it in a casual tone.

"I had just gotten there. I talked to Strommer on the phone not twenty minutes before that."

"Where did you call from?"

"A public booth."

Cielli seemed relieved. Dancey had no idea how difficult or easy it was to trace phone calls. "Let's hope that he didn't doodle while he spoke to you on the phone, Dancey."

"What were you doing there?"

"Looking for you. That should not surprise you. Was Strommer a friend of yours?"

"I knew him, yes. He worked at the Vatican Library."

"He had been making inquiries about you at the Columbus Hotel, by telephone, after your disappearance. It was one of the very few leads we had. Are you finished eating?"

Dancey had heaped a plate with doughnuts. Was it unnatural to have such an appetite in these circumstances? He shook his head to Cielli's question. Cielli was impatient. He looked around at the other tables, for the first time exhibiting open concern.

"I wish you'd hurry."

Dancey mumbled through a mouthful of doughnut, but Cielli's mood communicated itself to him.

Cielli leaned toward him. "What the hell is going on, Dancey? I know you're involved in something hush-hush at the Vatican Library. I know the government was willing to sweeten the pot to the tune of fifty thousand dollars. Is that money still in the bank?"

"Of course."

"So we had a dead porter and now we've got a dead librarian. Half the police in Lazio are looking for you. You want to eat, go ahead and eat, but between bites you better tell me what is going on or I can't be much help to you. Nobody can."

Had he subconsciously avoided going to the consulate so that he would not have to answer such questions? Dancey wanted to blurt it all out, as he had to Polly, but he could not. With Polly, it had been a matter of confiding to a friend, whereas to tell Cielli about the missing manuscript would be like an official report. His responsibility for it would then be a matter of record. And he had no illusions, after having told his story to Polly, that his version of what had happened would be found plausible.

"I can't tell you."

"Would you like me to ask Monsignor Nerone?"

"No!"

Cielli sat back and rubbed his eyes. "Listen to me, Dancey. I knew a man once, an American, who thought he could get out of the country with some Etruscan statuary. He was no crook. He wasn't even the president." Cielli smiled and stopped rubbing his eyes. "He had dug the stuff up in the yard of the house he was renting. All he knew was that it was valuable. Now, to the Italians, anything like that is a national treasure, part of the past, precious. This man figured he could get the stuff out of Italy. Dumb wops, you know. Dancey, he spent ten years in a prison near Naples. The embassy could do nothing. His hair fell out, his teeth went bad, in ten years he aged twenty. They locked the door and lost the key. That is how deeply they feel about such things in this country, Dancey. Coins. Statues. Manuscripts."

The point was made. Somehow Cielli knew of what he called the hush-hush project. Or was he simply conjecturing, putting together Strommer, the Vatican Library and Dancey's scholarship? And then it occurred to Dancey that the whole thing might be public knowledge now. He had not seen a newspaper yet.

"Was there anything in the paper?" he asked Cielli.

"About you? No. A small item on the porter's death." Cielli separated thumb and forefinger an inch and a half. "That's all. Don't take comfort from that. The man I told you about did not become news until the trial."

Dancey licked powdered sugar from his sticky fingers. His hunger was appeased. He could fear again.

"I want no confidences from you, Dancey. Just one answer. Have you stolen anything?"

"No."

"Could you be suspected of stealing something? You know the sort of thing I mean."

Dancey nodded.

120

Cielli played with his lips for a moment. "I meant it when I said nothing could be done for the man who tried to smuggle out the statues. Dancey, I am going to make an unorthodox suggestion. I did not find you in the street back there. We have not had this conversation. I am not going to the consulate. The best way I can help you is to get you out of the country. That's what I propose to do. Do you know Ostia? Good. Up the coastal road some twelve miles is a castle. I mean that. A castle. It was built by the Normans. I have an apartment there." Cielli took out a ring of keys and began to detach one from the rest. Dancey said nothing. He was sure it was the same castle he had seen with Polly. How many Norman castles are there near Rome?

"I want you to go there, Dancey. Take a cab to Ostia, then walk to the castle. You can follow the beach."

Dancey listened to the plan. Go to Cielli's castle apartment and soon be spirited out of the country. How appealing it was. He took the key. There was no point in telling Cielli he would not be going to the castle, at least not right away. He could not escape his responsibility for the Thomistic autograph that easily. Its loss had put Jacques in the hospital and Giuseppe and Strommer in the next world. And that manuscript was still missing. Grateful as he was to Cielli for his offer, he could not accept it.

Besides, it came too late. Dancey had become aware of a massive, gorilla-like man inside the café, at the bar, having his coffee standing. And keeping an eye on their table. Dancey had the eerie feeling that he was now seeing the pursuer he had fled from the night before as from an invisible adversary.

"Will you go there, Dancey?"

"Just take a cab to Ostia?"

"Any cab in this piazza will take you there. Do you have money?"

Dancey took the bills Cielli pressed into his hand. Why not? The gorilla at the counter watched the exchange. Dancey would have to go through the café in order to reach the street.

"Thanks, Cielli. I appreciate it."

Dancey rose suddenly. A woman and her dog vacated a nearby

table and started into the café. Dancey got next to her, so that she would be between him and the gorilla, and once inside, he made a break for the street door. Behind him there was a sudden terrified yapping. Dancey caught a backward glimpse of the big man, his feet twisted in the dog's leash, crashing to the floor. The woman's scream, the barking of the dog, the instant pandemonium this created, gave Dancey a head start.

16

Dancey was not reluctant to run when he nipped out of the café. He darted across the street, maneuvering among the lanes of traffic, and ran for a full block, flat out. He stopped then and turned and saw a huge figure come into sight. If he had not stopped, he might not have been seen. Around the corner then, he broke into a run, going up the side street like a flash, hoping he looked like your average demented jogger. There was a church ahead and he made for it as if sanctuary were still an operative concept.

It was a new church, with a high ceiling that looked like poured concrete. The walls had an intentionally rough, unfinished look. Dancey moved right up the main aisle toward the altar, which was set in the intersection of the cruciform edifice. He stopped in front of it as if the flickering red lamp were a traffic signal. To the right was the sacristy. At a small altar on the far side of the nave, a man who would be the sacristan was puttering with a bank of vigil lights before a statue. Dancey hurried into the sacristy, running on tiptoe. It smelled of incense and wax and linen, a churchy smell. He pulled open a cabinet and, on a sudden inspiration, stepped inside and closed the door after him.

Garments, vestments, hung all around him, and he pushed through them to the back of the closet. It was hot and airless and uncomfortable—he could not stand fully erect—but at that moment it seemed a little bit of heaven. Minutes went by, then more. Dancey was willing to remain there for the rest of the day if necessary. He thought of Cielli's offer to get him out of the country, and tried to convince himself that he might have taken him up on it if that man had not shown up at the café counter. Maybe, if he could elude him . . .

And then he heard what had to be that big man's voice. He was talking to the sacristan. A man? What man? The sacristan had seen no one. A silence. Money being passed? The sacristan was grateful but, unfortunately, he had not seen a man come into the church. What did he look like? The question was ignored. How many ways out of the church are there? As Dancey had suspected, there were half a dozen exits.

"All open?"

"During the day? Of course. This is a church."

"What's that there?"

"The sacristy. Who are you?"

"I am pursuing a fugitive," the voice said primly. "Is there a door in there too?"

"From the sacristy? Of course. It goes into the cloister. Where the priests live," the sacristan added, as if he felt the other might need the explanation.

Dancey heard footsteps come into the sacristy. They went by his closet. A door opened. "You see," the sacristan said. His voice had lowered.

The footsteps returned, seemed to hesitate for a moment, and then went rapidly away. Dancey could hear the sacristan's profane muttering. Obviously the big man had left. Sweat was running off Dancey, and not simply because of the cramped heat of the closet. The garments hanging all around him were heavy. And long. He ran his fingers down a line of buttons. Ah.

Some ten minutes went past before there were no longer any sounds in the sacristy. The sacristan, talking nonstop to himself, had banged a pail, run water and scrubbed the floor—guesses in the dark closet which were subsequently verified—and Dancey was certain the man must now open the closet and discover him, when a small bell rang. Sounds of going. Dancey waited. The sacristan returned. Someone wanted to go to confession.

"Wait in the confessional, signora. The bell rings in the cloister. A father will come."

"I want Father Cornelio," a querulous voice said.

"He is not on duty today."

"Tell him I wish to confess to him. I am sure he will come."

"A father will come. Wait in the confessional, signora."

What sounded like the snap of a purse, then rustling. "*Grazie*, signora. *Grazie*. I will go speak to Father Cornelio. Go into the church and wait."

Footsteps went away in different directions. Dancey heard a door open and shut. The cloister? He pushed at the closet door with his foot and stayed back among the cassocks. For that is what the garments were, the cassocks put on by boys when they served at Mass. There was no reaction to the opening of the closet door, so he stepped out. His hair was damp and plastered to his head with sweat. He felt as if he had just played tennis. When he turned to look into the closet, his heart dropped. The cassocks were red. He opened the door wider and began to sort through them, like a matron at a sale. And then, thank God, he saw that there were some black cassocks too. He took the longest one he could find and held it against his body. Good enough. He slipped into it and began to button up. The row of buttons rose from toe to throat. Buttoning with one hand, he opened the next cabinet. A biretta, the three-winged headpiece worn by priests in church, hung on a hook. He decided against it. In another closet, on an upper shelf, was a dusty black wide-brimmed hat, of the kind worn on the street.

Buttoned up, the hat on his head, he needed a collar. He looked around for a piece of cardboard or paper, anything to suggest a clerical collar. He began to open drawers. Some copies of Mass leaflets. He took one. It was dated for the following Sunday, June 27. He turned it over, looking for blank white. There was only the margin. It would have to do. He folded the leaflet several times and inserted it into the collar of the cassock. Time to go.

When he went into the church, a thin, bony woman half rose

from a pew, looking at Dancey with alarm. He stopped. What the hell was wrong? The sight of Dancey seemed both to frighten and to anger her.

"I want Father Cornelio," she snapped.

"He will be with you shortly, signora. Please be seated."

He swept past her toward the street door he had entered by. Easing it open, he saw the big man standing outside on the steps. He looked lost. He also looked determined. Apparently his orders had run out on him, but he looked as if he might just wait right there for new ones. His tenacity did nothing to reassure Dancey.

He retraced his steps up the aisle, ignoring the return of alarm to the fussy penitent. When he drew abreast of the sacristy, he heard voices, the sacristan's and another. Dancey ducked into a pew, knelt and lowered his face into his hands. It occurred to him that he should not be wearing the hat. When he took it off, he stole a glance at the sacristan and the old priest with him. The woman rose to her feet, burbling with delight, but the priest looked anything but delighted to see her.

"Again?" he said despairingly.

Dancey did not speculate what it was whose repetition dismayed the old priest: her being there or what she might be there to confess. The sacristan had noticed him take off the hat and now stood staring at him. On impulse, Dancey beckoned the man to him. And the sacristan came, if somewhat reluctantly.

"Father?"

Dancey stood and brought the hat up between them, to conceal his makeshift collar.

"I want you to call the police."

"The police!" His eyes darted toward Father Cornelio and the woman, but they were headed for a confessional. The sacristan shook his head as if to clear it. Obviously his job seldom afforded him the kind of interruptions he was getting today.

"The police," Dancey repeated firmly. "There is a wanted man standing in front of the church. He is ... " Dancey touched his head and rolled his eyes. He described the big man. Recognition

126

shone in the sacristan's eyes. Such a man had been inside the church, in the sacristy.

"I know. I know. He is running through the streets looking for John the Baptist. Did he ask for him?"

"John the Baptist!"

Dancey nodded. "The poor man. At first we thought it was a case of diabolical possession. He is extremely strong and very determined to find John the Baptist. I doubt that you and I could subdue him."

The sacristan quickly agreed. "I will call the police. Do you want to come with me, Father?"

"I will stay here. To guard the church."

The sacristan hurried off through the sacristy and into the cloister. Dancey rounded the main altar and headed for a far door. When he stepped outside, he was only six feet from an ice cream wagon parked at the curb. It was surrounded by shouting kids. Suddenly the thought of an ice cream cone seemed more desirable than safety itself. After his stay in the sacristy closet, he was all but dehydrated. Dancey dug out a coin and waved it over the heads of the kids, catching the vendor's eye.

"Che vuole, padre?"

"Vorrei un gelato, per favore."

The kids grumbled and complained, but Dancey ignored the little anticlericals. Just then he would have gone mano a mano with his massive pursuer for that cone. And in a moment he had it, pressed down and running over.

He clamped the hat on his head and, licking his cone with abandon, began to move at a swift but clerical clip up an avenue lined with apartment buildings of the lower middle class. It was, he found, the Via Ugo Balzani. He knew where he was, but he did not know where it was in relation to anything else. The street ended, its mouth facing a row of shops. To the right was open countryside, lovely hills dotted with villas. He went to the left, up a hill, again to the right and some minutes later found himself, he knew not how, on the Via Nomentana. He finished his ice cream cone, hailed a cab and told the driver to take him to the Borgo Santo Spirito.

He sank back in the seat, his mind a blank. With relief came thoughts of Cielli's plan for his safety. All he had to do was to change his order, tell the driver to head for Ostia. The thought lay on his mind like a fallen leaf. Poor Strommer. And poor Jacques too. Dancey was the only one still on his feet. Unless he counted Nerone.

The image of that prelate formed in his mind, as he had first seen him in the Italian Embassy in Washington, as Nerone had looked across the table when they had lunch in the Trattoria Posti, as he had seen him from the window of Mrs. Parson's room directing the search for Giuseppe, as he had seen him in the hallway when he was all dolled up for his escape. The same face, different expressions. What was he up to? A priest, a monsignor, involved in theft and murder? Well, damn it, why not? Think of Chaucer, think of Boccaccio, think of Dante. *Corruptio optimi pessima:* the bigger they are, the harder they fall. Fall. Strommer. Good God. His body in the street, covered with a blanket. Dancey could still hear Strommer's bleating voice on the telephone. He could not remember whether heavy bodies fall faster than light ones. Of course they do, except in a vacuum. He felt that he himself was moving in a vacuum of a sort, not part of the ordinary world, though he seemed to be.

He noticed the driver's eyes framed in the rear-view mirror like an oculist's ad. They shifted slightly and the two men's gazes met. The driver looked away. Dancey touched his neck and found that the Mass leaflet had popped free, its corner up under his ear. He had need of a more convincing Roman collar.

He stopped the cab as soon as it turned into the Borgo, paid the driver, and went into a stationery store, where he asked for an envelope.

"One?" The proprietor's look of hope, stirred by Dancey's entrance, went into eclipse.

Dancey repeated that he wanted an envelope, a large one. White. It cost ten lire. The poor devil. Dancy selected a ballpoint

128

pen from a box on the counter, bringing his bill to a hundred lire, but the clerk's hopeful look had gone for good. In the street outside, Dancey carefully folded the crisp white envelope lengthwise. He put the Mass leaflet in his pocket and donned his new collar. Better. Much better. He even felt more clerical. A beautiful young woman passed, nodding deferentially to him. He touched the brim of his hat. Bless you, my dear. Boccaccio indeed. But he had succeeded in not waggling his brows.

Dancey strolled up the street on the north sidewalk, and when he saw the entrance of the building on the opposite side, he kept going, continuing for fifty yards before crossing and coming back. Taking a deep breath, he plunged through the entrance and headed purposefully toward the *portiere's* cubicle. The man was poring over a much-thumbed copy of *Playboy,* and, when he looked up, his mouth fell open and he tried to shove the magazine out of sight. Dancey let his eyes rest on the newspaper under which the offensive periodical had been ineffectively hidden. It did no harm to have the *portiere* on the defensive. Who knew what sweaty hours in the confessional Dancey's cassocked figure conjured up for him?

"Monsignor Nerone sent me."

"Yes, Father. What is it?"

Dancey took off his hat and brought it to his breast. "Of course you heard what happened to Giuseppe."

"*Madre di Dio,*" the *portiere* cried, crossing himself with a swift fly-shooing gesture. His expression told Dancey nothing. His mouth continued to hang open. So did his jacket, a sort of uniform coat with metal buttons.

"What did you hear?"

The *portiere* seemed to have trouble grasping what Dancey meant.

"Did Giuseppe come here yesterday?" There was a chair next to the table. Dancey sat down and put his hand on the newspaper that imperfectly hid the magazine. The man's eyes never left Dancey's hand.

"What do you want to know?"

129

Dancey sighed, the soul of patience, and steepled his fingers. He felt like Barry Fitzgerald. "Everything."

"But I told the monsignor."

"I know you did. And now I want you to tell me." Dancey kept time to his words by tapping his fingers on the newspaper. "Giuseppe came here yesterday, bringing something to the studio."

"What studio is that, Father?"

"What is the name of the place?" He closed his eyes and feigned deep thought. There was the sound of the newspaper and magazine being whipped away. When Dancey opened his eyes, the *portiere* was pathetically eager to be of help. "A photographic studio of some kind," Dancey said.

"Not in this building."

"Of course in this building." He stood. "Come with me."

"But I can't do that, Father. I have to stay here."

Dancey walked around the table and stared at the magazine sticking out of the wastebasket. "You should take out your trash. Come with me."

The *portiere* came with him. They went through the first courtyard and into the second. Dancey's head was ahum with memories. They walked to the door out of which Luigi and Teresa had come to meet him on the day the procedure had been explained to Dancey. Inside, on the first floor, were the offices of a minor publisher. A dressmaker's establishment, a sweatshop by the look of it, was on the second floor. Pretty but cowed girls looked up from their work and down again, fearful of the boss or put off, perhaps, by the goatish gleam in the *portiere's* eye.

"The top floor is empty," he told Dancey.

"Show me."

"I assure you, Father, it is empty." The man was recovering from the embarrassment of being caught looking at dirty pictures by a priest.

"A man and a woman . . . "

"Ah!" The *portiere's* eyes suddenly glazed. "Of course. I remember. They did ask to see that floor and the woman did mention a studio. An artist, I suppose." He licked his lips. "She must have been his model."

Lust glowed like foxfire in the *portiere's* eyes. Could he mean Teresa? Dancey recalled Luigi's slovenly aide. If the *portiere's* desire could be stirred by her, it seemed clinical evidence of the pernicious effects of pornography.

"You found her attractive?"

They started up the stairs to the next floor. For answer, the *portiere* wagged his head helplessly and threw out his arms.

"You see," he said, when they reached the top of the stairs. The large room he pointed to was indeed empty. It was from its window that Luigi and Teresa had looked out.

"The woman you showed this to . . . " Dancey began.

"Yes," the *portiere* sighed.

"Describe her to me."

For a man who whiled away his time studying photographs of women, the *portiere* showed an abysmal inability to describe one. But then Dancey had asked about her face.

"I must return to my post," the *portiere* said, stern duty tugging him from lubricious memory.

Dancey had to accept the incredible fact that there was no photographic lab in this building, no place where microfiching might be done. The implications of the fact were enormous and vertiginous. Anger and confusion welled up in him. He told the *portiere* to return to his lodge. He wanted a moment to think.

But think about what? This empty room mocked him, delivered no explanation, rendered all his memories dubious. He had come here with the notion that by backtracking from the intended destination of the Thomistic manuscript, he would be able to form some idea of what had gone wrong. The lack of a studio for microfiching manuscripts effectively removed the ground from under all his assumptions of what he had been engaged upon.

Some minutes later, passing the empty lodge, Dancey stopped. The *portiere's* jacket was draped over the back of a chair. Dancey darted inside, stepped out of the cassock, plopped it and his broad-brimmed hat on the desk, and, in a moment, was heading for the street, pulling on the *portiere's* jacket as he went.

17

Another surprise awaited him in the Borgo Santo Spirito. He could not find the office of Dr. Piero Lancia. Perhaps the absence of the microfiche studio prepared him for this second lacuna, at least to some degree, for his incredulity was less. At the door where there should have been a brass plate—surely he had seen such a plate when he had entered, conscious of Cielli's watchful eyes upon him as he dutifully reported for his physical and cholera shot—there was nothing. Such brass plates as he did find announced the premises of lawyers and real estate agents and dentists. Gaudier signs informed the passer-by of the presence of hairdressers and modistes. And, inevitably, of several wigmakers.

Not finding the office the first time, making a random pass, he became systematic, triangulating with reference to the building he had just left, the garage doors behind which was the stone statue of St. Francis, and zeroing in on ... nothing. Well, on a lawyer's office. While he was doing this, he half expected the *portiere* to come rushing into the street in quest of his missing jacket. Fortunately, this did not happen before Dancey was sure he had found, brass plate or no brass plate, the door he had entered to see Lancia. From the corner of his eye he saw the *portiere*, in the middle of the street now, stopping traffic, waving a cassock with one hand and interrogating the universe with a clenched fist. Dancey, shielded from the *portiere* by the door he opened, stepped inside.

A cool quiet hallway with a marble floor. A ledgelike table emerging from the wall, on it a vase of huge odorous flowers, behind it a great gilt-framed mirror in which Dancey saw a somewhat bewildered menial peering back at him. A *portiere*? His beardless self. A sound of voices, women's voices, coming toward him. The agitated chirping tones seemed to emphasize that this was a home, not an office, he had entered. His presence here would surely precipitate a scene. But he could not move. Outside was that goddam *portiere* and the promise of another, probably worse scene. Theft or housebreaking; which was worse? It seemed a fine point. In his favor, it seemed, was the fact that the street door had not been locked.

Heels on the marble floor, the voices louder, and then, out of a doorway, both speaking at once, two women appeared, matronly, absorbed in themselves. Middle-aged, imperious, they had the easy authority of wealth and position. Even in his panic, Dancey realized that he was invisible to them. What were they chattering about?

One of the women, her hair tinted a lovely unnatural color and piled high upon her head, carried a box. Somehow she noticed Dancey without looking directly at him.

"So. You are here. Take it."

She thrust the box into Dancey's hand.

"Tell Laura I am furious. Insulted. It is not at all what I wanted. My day is ruined. I had planned to wear the dress this afternoon, and now ... " Her voice caught, as if on a sob.

"Francesca," the other woman said. "Wear the blue silk. It becomes you. You are beautiful in it."

Francesca's sobbing seemed genuine. She permitted the other woman to embrace her. A many-ringed hand patted the heaving shoulders in consolation. Steely eyes glared at Dancey.

"Go. Take it. Be off."

He went. He took it. He was off. In the street, the box proved a shield of sorts. He held it high before him and sailed up the street. He had lost interest in finding Lancia's office. It he was going to find some touchstone, it would not be in the Borgo Santo Spirito. The fingertip that had been pricked for blood throbbed; the arm that had been impaled on Lancia's choleric needle ached. What was real and what unreal?

Money is real. Fifty-five thousand dollars is real. If there was no microfiche project, to what had the government donated all that money? The role of infuriated taxpayer seemed as good as any now. He would withdraw that money lest, somehow, it got into the wrong hands. But of course, as much as anything, he had to find out if his visit to the bank had been illusory too.

When Dancey arrived at the teller's window in the Banco di Roma after a ten-minute wait in line, a period during which he had the unsettling opportunity to review the discrepancies between his memories and the tangible world, he stared across the counter at the man. Though he nestled the box in his arms, the buttons on his coat must have effectively placed him for his fellow proletarian.

"Sì, compagno?"

Dancey pulled his passbook from the pocket where, together with his wallet and passport, it had been in warm relation with his thigh. "I wish to withdraw . . . " He hesitated. All of it? If not all, then now much? "I wish to withdraw fifty thousand dollars."

Raised in a tradition where bankers are sedate and bloodless, Dancey was not ready for the shout of surprise that greeted his request. "Feefty tousand dolors!" The imperfect echo of his words told him that he had spoken English. The heads of other tellers turned toward the astounded functionary, whose eyes stared in a popped fashion through a pair of tinted glasses.

"There is my book. You will notice the deposit."

The teller with the tinted glasses snatched up the book and paged through it. He was soon joined by colleagues who abandoned their clients in order to examine this incredible passbook. Surely some of them must recognize him from his visit here with Cielli. But Dancey would have hesitated to pick any of them out of a line-up, if it came to that. The thought of a line-up made him wish he had not had the mad idea to rescue from misuse the money of the harried American taxpayer. And then he remembered the *direttore.*

"Take me to your *direttore,*" he cried.

"Take him to Ponzi. Take him to the *direttore.*" The tellers took up the chant like a Greek chorus. A section of the counter was lifted, Dancey stepped through and went with Tinted Glasses to

135

office of the *direttore*. Signor Ponzi seemed to be asleep with his eyes open.

"This *signore* wishes to withdraw fifty thousand dollars," the teller announced in a tone that would have done service as the last trump.

Ponzi rose from his chair as if an electric current had begun to course through it. He slapped his temples with open hands and then lifted them to heaven. The teller prodded Dancey into the office, where he came to a stop before Ponzi's desk.

"Who are you?" the *direttore* snapped, eyes narrowed. "How many of you are there?"

"I am a client of this bank," Dancey said, dropping the passbook on the desk. "I wish to make a withdrawal."

The *direttore* examined the passbook with fastidious disdain, using a letter opener to open it. *"Il suo passaporto, per favore."*

Dancey was congratulating himself on having thought to take his passport with him when he left Polly's until he remembered his absence of beard. Having flipped open the passport, Ponzi let his eyes travel from photograph to Dancey to photograph again. He slapped the green folder with the back of his hand. "This is not your passport."

"Of course it's my passport."

Ponzi flicked his chin with the side of his hand. "The beard. You have no beard."

"I shaved it off."

Ponzi emitted a brief barking laugh. "It is not you."

"I am James Dancey. That is my passport. This is my passbook. I deposited fifty-five thousand dollars in this bank a few days ago. I wish to withdraw thirty thousand dollars."

Did he actually think that dropping the amount would cushion the blow? What a mistake this had been. Ponzi would call in the police. Dancey realized that he was still hugging the box that had been thrust upon him by the disconsolate Francesca. He placed it carefully on Ponzi's desk. If he had to make a quick exit, he did not want to be encumbered by that box.

"You wish to withdraw thirty thousand dollars?" Ponzi fell back in his chair. "Just like that. Do you think I am in the habit of

136

turning money over to strangers? Write your name on that paper."

He pushed a slip of paper toward Dancey, who sat and scrawled his signature. If worse came to worse, he would demand they call the consulate. Cielli would come to his assistance. Dear God, why had he not taken a cab to Ostia? He might have been there by now, walking up the beach toward the Norman castle, gulls crying, the sound of the surf, the sun. He would have liked to sob, like Francesca.

Ponzi compared the signature Dancey had just made with that in the passbook. He smiled malevolently. Their evident similarity proved nothing. Papers were called for and papers were brought, papers Dancey had signed at this very desk. More comparisons. Ponzi pushed another piece of paper across the desk. "Write your name again."

"What is this, best two out of three?"

"Eh?"

He wrote his name again. Ponzi compared this new entry with the others and then, apparently convinced against his will, let out a great despairing sigh. "You have shaved off your beard."

"Yes."

"Signor Dancey, you must understand my caution. This account." He slapped the papers before him. "I made it clear when you opened it that it was a *conto personale*. Only you can make a withdrawal."

"I understand."

"Monsignor Nerone does not. He seemed to think it was a joint account."

"Did he come here?"

"He sent somebody. I refused. I had to refuse. Afterward, the monsignor telephoned." Ponzi passed a hand across his face, then left it there, looking as if over a fan at Dancey. He made a blatting sound into the palm of his hand, crossing his eyes as he did so. Dancey got the idea.

"When was this?"

Ponzi looked at his watch. Not two hours ago.

"Signor Ponzi, I doubt that the man who came here was an emissary from Monsignor Nerone. I doubt that it was Monsignor

137

Nerone who spoke rudely to you on the telephone."

Dancey had no idea where these certainties came from or if indeed he had them. The effect of his words on Ponzi was mixed. Horror that he might have been persuaded to cut a few corners at the behest of a soi-disant Vatican dignitary, relief that he had turned over no money. The thought of escaping money brought his thoughts back to Dancey.

"You want thirty thousand dollars?" His hand went to his heart. He looked stern. "Naturally, I must give it to you in lire."

"That's all right."

"And the rest will stay in the bank?" Ponzi's manner was brightening.

"For the time being."

Ponzi, firm in the banker's belief that money must be kept from even its rightful possessor, and if not all of it, then as much as possible, effected the withdrawal in a trice, as trices are measured in the Italian banking community.

"You will carry it in that box?" Ponzi indicated the package Dancey had been given by the doleful Francesca.

Nodding, Dancey slipped aside the string and eased the top off the box. Ponzi, pitching in, reached across and pulled back the tissue paper. A dress was revealed, peach-colored, filmy. The *direttore* was surprised.

"Francesca didn't like it," Dancey explained. He took some of the material with two fingers and caressed it with the ball of his thumb. "It is simply not her color."

"It is a lovely color."

"Thank you. Just put it in."

Ponzi laid the lovely lire atop the lovely dress. Dancey arranged the tissue paper and slipped the cover onto the box. He retied the string as if he had all the time in the world.

Eventually he was on his way. As he headed for the street, he told himself he would be back. If money meant for a nonexistent microfiching project was going to fall into the wrong hands, he intended those hands to be his own.

138

18

With his arms full of taxpayers' money and a pocket crammed with Cielli's contribution to cab fare, Dancey could not afford a phone call until he bought a *gettone*. He effected this transaction in a *tabaccheria* on the Corso Vittorio Emanuele, whither he went on foot, crossing the bridge of the same name. Having dialed Polly's number, he stood listening to it ring and looked around the little shop. A brisk business in salt and stamps and cigarettes. Dancey moved the dress box under his arm, and rested it on his hip. Across the store an eyebrow raised. Dancey shifted his hip into a lower gear. He had to remember he was no longer sailing under an alien registry. The sound of Polly's ringing phone continued in his ear. He continued to listen to it because contacting Polly exhausted the plans with which he had entered the *tabaccheria*. Where the hell was she?

He hung up and, hugging his box of money, went into the street. Right or left, what the hell did it matter; he had no idea where he was headed. How would Polly spend a day that had begun with the unannounced departure of her uninvited overnight guest? He imagined her, loaded down with newspapers and pastry, returning to the empty apartment. An expression of abject disappointment on her imagined face seemed unrealistic. Surprise, yes. Disappointment, maybe. Anger, almost certainly. Would it even occur to her that he had left in order to remove from her apartment the danger he represented? Probably not. How much of his wild story had she even half believed?

The sun stood high in the sky now and the traffic vied with itself to reach a more passionate pitch of chaos. A bus's tires mounted the curb and pressed the pedestrians closer to the buildings as it plowed on through fumes and dusty sunlight. All semblance of feeling for fellow sufferers had deserted the crowds on the sidewalk. Shelley said that hell is a city very much like London, or was it the other way around? At the moment, Rome was purgatorial at best. These people visibly longed to be out of its heat, its press and push. At the beach? Ostia.

The *portiere's* jacket was hot and redolent of ancient perspiration, ignited by the heat. Dancey slipped it off. His clothes were, if wrinkled, nonetheless dry now. A Gypsy in a long dress, baby draped over one arm, accosted him. He gave her the *portiere's* coat. She was the first surprised Gypsy Dancey had ever seen, but her indecision was brief. Clutching the coat, she disappeared, making a grab for the box as well, but Dancey had been ready for that. Grand larceny is catching. Why the hell was he walking around Rome carrying thirty thousand dollars' worth of lire and a dress that had ruined Francesca's day?

He tried Polly's number again, without result. How did she spend any day? She had spoken of sketching. And there was her uncle. Gainer! The thought of the old man drove away the attractions of Ostia and escape. Gainer had been his father's friend; it did not matter that he had checked up on Dancey to see if he really was a medievalist working at the Vatican Library. That bespoke just the kind of level-headed common sense Dancey was desperately in need of at the moment.

"Who did you ask about me?" Dancey asked some twenty minutes later, seated at Gainer's luncheon table, enjoying his salmon and Frascati.

"Ulrich Strommer. Do you know him?"

Even the best of wines, swallowed wrongly, will make one choke. Dancey covered his empurpled face with a napkin and looked a tearful apology to his host.

"Drink some water," Gainer advised. "Ulrich and I get along; he

140

understands me. If he were in charge down there, my life in Rome would be more pleasant than it is. But Jacques is my nemesis. He sees me as an enemy. He begrudges me even so much as a look at his precious manuscripts."

Dancey, recovered, expressed surprise at this. Gainer smiled a rueful smile.

"My fault as much as his. One day when he was fussing over my shoulder down there, worried about the manuscript I was looking at, I offered to buy the damned thing from him. Or rent it. Anything to be able to study it without him haunting me."

"You weren't serious."

"I'm always serious when I make an offer. Of course, I had no illusion Jacques would take me up on it. What I didn't bargain for was his lasting distrust. Ulrich Strommer is another sort of man entirely."

It was eerie listening to Gainer speak of Strommer in the present tense, but Dancey, safe in this cool, luxurious apartment, was reluctant to begin his tale of woe. Gainer wielded the silverware with his large spotted hands, worrying the food, sipping a little wine, a garrulous old fellow perhaps, but with a wildcatter's wily wisdom still. Dancey was certain he had come to the right man.

"I've heard talk of a project to microfiche the entire manuscript collection," Dancey said.

"Jacques opposes it."

"It sounded like a good idea," Dancey said weakly.

"It is a good idea." Gainer took a sip of water, then revolved the glass slowly, setting off a faint chiming of ice cubes. "They are going through with it, too."

"Did Strommer tell you that?"

Gainer looked at him sharply, then smiled. "Putting two and two together, are you? If I said yes, I'd be betraying a trust, now wouldn't I? And if I said no, you wouldn't believe me."

Dancey felt dismal. Gainer no longer seemed someone he could lean upon. Apparently Strommer had duped him too with the story of a go-ahead on the microfiche project. To what purpose?

"Mr. Gainer, Strommer is dead."

141

Gainer became immobile, but his expression was that of a man who has reached the age where news of death can no longer surprise.

"How do you know that?"

"He died this morning. He fell from his balcony into the street. Maybe he was pushed."

"Pushed!"

"Do you know Ernesto Cielli?"

"That sonofabitch," Gainer said emphatically. "Cielli pushed Strommer off his balcony?"

"Cielli? No, of course not!"

"You think he wouldn't do it if there was a dime in it for him? You don't know Cielli very well."

Dancey's estimate of Gainer's common sense plummeted. Did the old man seriously think that a man connected with the American consulate would do a thing like that?

"Son, let me tell you about Ernesto Cielli."

What the story told Dancey was that Gainer was a snob. It was not that Cielli was in trade that bothered the old man. It was not his money either. Apparently Cielli could buy and sell most of the Americans in Rome who were amused at the profit he turned importing trampolines, styrofoam buckets, condoms, and dashboard compasses. Junk, Gainer said. Five-and-dime stuff, the staple of the discount house. Nonetheless, it had made Cielli rich. He had a farm in Umbria, a house in Rome, and an apartment by the sea. He had a boat and a fleet of cars. What Gainer did not like were Cielli's morals. He had—though he had thought this a secret—two common-law wives, nine children and a mistress besides.

"Doesn't he work at the consulate?"

"Sure he does." Gainer seemed to feel this strengthened his point. "The amateur diplomat. The rich volunteer. They love that sort of thing on the Via Veneto. That isn't why I hate the bastard."

"Oh."

"Polly. He had the nerve to make a play for Polly. Can you imagine that? I called him in and put a stop to it. I told him there were impediments. Know what he said?" Gainer gulped some wine. "The sonofabitch said, 'I understood she was divorced.' Well, I told him the impediments weren't on Polly's side. That shut him up, let me tell you. He seemed to think all those households he maintains were a secret."

"What did Polly think of this?"

"Now, what do you suppose she thought?"

Dancey knew what he hoped her reaction had been. Cielli and Polly? It was ludicrous. Gainer's attitude toward Cielli no longer seemed snobbish. Why, Cielli was twice as old as Polly.

"Ever since, I've been waiting for Cielli to take his revenge on me. He will, someday, I don't know how. He never forgets, he never forgives. And he is ruthless. Sometimes I think he feels toward the old U. S. of A. the way he feels toward me. The man isn't an American and he isn't a proper Italian either. You see why I don't find it far-fetched that Cielli would shove a man off a balcony?"

That had to set some sort of record for the non sequitur. Dancey blinked. "What did he have to do with Strommer?"

"There must be something. Come on. I'll show you my study."

Nathaniel Gainer had two complete sets of Migne's *Latin Patrology*, one at the ranch outside Midland, the other in his study in Rome. He had only one set of the *Corpus Scriptorum Ecclesiasticorum Latinorum*. He had Baemker's *Beitraege*. His library was a medievalist's dream, the fulfillment of the dream he had first fashioned as an undergraduate at Oxford. He was happy to speak of these things to Dancey. In the beginning, he admitted, the dream had been partly defensive. Beneath the veneer of British politeness, he had detected disdain for the scion of a Texas oilman, no matter that his classical training at Fordham prep rivaled that obtainable at the best English schools. While the English curriculum swung toward the dominant American model, Gainer had vowed to dedicate himself to the older educational ideal. Contact with Campion House and Ronald Knox removed any sense of inferiority at being Catholic. After all, he wasn't Irish. Renewed pride in his religion turned him to the Middle Ages. He became an

143

accomplished scholar and an avid collector of medievalia.

Dancey was impressed. Ensconced in his study, having reviewed his life, Gainer permitted the news of Strommer's death to affect him.

"I liked that man, Dancey. He had given his life to scholarship. Who could blame him if, from time to time, nearing the age of sixty, he sometimes looked back with a little regret? He was a good medievalist, but his favorite author was Horace. You know the story of the Sabine farm. Strommer had come to share that love of land, that passion for a spot of earth to call his own."

"Which he couldn't afford?"

"Do you find my reaction to his death surprising? The fact is, I am not surprised. Ulrich had become involved in things that are dangerous."

"What do you mean?" Dancey sat forward. Had the conversation unexpectedly come round to where he could enlist Gainer's help and ask his advice? The old man's tale about Cielli had cast doubt on the wisdom of making for the Norman castle.

Gainer pulled a large volume toward him across his desk. "Do you know this? The Leonine edition of Thomas Aquinas's commentary on the Book of Job. A beautiful piece of work."

"What sort of dangerous things?" Dancey asked.

"*De mortuis nil nisi bonum.* Speak well of the dead."

"Mr. Gainer, we might be speaking of the same thing. You know why I'm in Rome."

"You have a scholarship. You're working at the Vatican Library."

"That's true. But do you know what else? Strommer told me about the microfiche program too. He asked me to help on it."

The phone on the desk rang at the same time as the doorbell. Gainer remarked that Caterina could not handle both, and picked up the phone. He listened intently, his face darkening.

"You sonofabitch!" he shouted, and slammed down the phone. He swung on Dancey.

"That was Ernesto Cielli."

"What did he want?"

"To sell me something, something that connects him with Strommer's death."

Dancey waited.

"A Thomistic autograph. Part of the *Summa contra gentiles*. Of course it's stolen."

Caterina appeared in the doorway, indicating that Gainer was wanted. The old man, fuming, muttering, got to his feet and shuffled out of the study. Dancey too got up. He went to the desk and looked down at Thomas's commentary on Job. I alone have escaped to tell you? The sound of voices came to him. Apprehension drew him from the study. He went down the hall and stepped into the dining room. The box containing the lire and the rejected dress lay on the sideboard. He picked it up. He had recognized the voice of the man with whom Gainer was speaking.

"Come with me, Bruno," Gainer said. "He's in the study."

They passed the dining room door, Gainer and the massive man who had chased Dancey from the Piazza Bologna that morning. Dancey stiffened to a statue, and when they turned into the hallway leading to the study, he darted from the dining room and ran to the front door. He got it open and turned to look into the startled face of Caterina, who was emerging from the kitchen.

"Thanks for lunch," Dancey said.

And then he was in the hall, pulling the door shut after him. As he had hoped, the elevator was on this floor. Its door hissed shut after him, he punched the bottom button and sank swiftly downward to the garage, the street, and the renewal of flight.

19

He rode down the Via Archimede on the back of a delivery truck that took the curves and winding descent at forty miles an hour, making it difficult for him to hang on to the truck as well as the box of money. On the Via Flaminia, he caught a bus and sat on the upper deck. He got off at the Piazza del Popolo, where he sat at a sidewalk table and ordered beer. His table was almost in the traffic lane and he meditatively kicked the rear tire of a temporarily stalled car. As if in response, it moved ahead a few feet. The desperate honking of jammed automobiles filled the air. The noise seemed the objective correlative of his own angry frustration.

His proximity to Polly's apartment made it a great temptation to go there. It was hot in the square . . . the beer did not help. He had run out of people to whom he could turn. Strommer was dead; Cielli was worse than Gainer had described him: perhaps he really was responsible for Strommer's death. If that was true, the confusion Dancey had felt at discovering there was no microfiche studio and no office of Dr. Piero Lancia was twice confounded. Gainer's chummy familiarity with the gorilla who had scared hell out of him that morning made him an inadvisable refuge.

The beer, added to Frascati, fatigue and fear, made him giddy. He looked around at the other tables with a grin on his face. If horns are the emblem of the cuckold, what crown could he wear to inform the world that he was a prize ass? He turned back to the traffic and to his thoughts. Reflections in a house of mirrors. What in the name of God was going on? He did not have a clue.

He ordered another beer and gulped it down. As it had the week after he received his doctorate, drunkenness beckoned, oblivion in a sea of troubles. Around him tourists were chattering in a tangle of tongues. Sightseers. Vacationers. Carefree wanderers. How he envied them. He rose from the table, scattered money on it, and set off. He was seized by the desire to stroll. He had been chased around Rome too goddam much. Surely he had earned the right to see the city as a tourist. *Nos qui morituri . . .*

Ten minutes later, he was on the Spanish Steps, watching representatives of international hippiedom twisting wire into more of the bogus jewelry displayed on cloths before them. He smelled the flowers. He basked in the sun. He mounted to the Pincio, where he strolled the graveled walks of the Villa Medici. He took a cab to the Piazza Navona, where he ordered half a liter of wine and lazed in the square.

His eyes lifted to the huge figures in the fountain, went beyond to the façade of a church, ceased to focus or register the external world. Thoughts of his parents, thoughts of ten years ago, flooded his mind. Remembered joy, the recollection of the three of them together, his father and mother and himself, caught in his throat. It was all gone now. He could not return to that Rome. It was no longer there.

His eyes focused. The same setting, buildings, streets, piazzas, statuary, had witnessed a constant turnover in the cast of human characters. How impermanent men are compared with their arti-facts. He had been in this square with his parents. This identical place. Doubtless it would still be here a hundred years from now, a mute commentary on the short-lived hopes of men.

The sense of mortality turned his mind to Père Jacques and he was back in Wonderland again, where nothing was what it seemed. The enigmatic Roberto Nerone; Giuseppe and Strommer dead. He telephoned Salvator Mundi, the hospital on the Janicu-lum hill, and, claiming to be calling on Monsignor Nerone's behalf, was told that the priest's condition was unchanged. Dancey felt that if only he could talk to Jacques, to someone he could trust, he might be able to figure out what the hell was going on.

The thought of just taking off occurred to him. He could hitch-hike through Austria and catch a flight from Munich. Would he encounter any difficulty if he just took a bus out to Fiumicino and boarded a plane for home? It did not matter. He could not go. He was prevented from going by the Vatican manuscript, the Thomistic autograph. It had to be returned to the Vatican Library. That much at least he could do for Jacques, and for Strommer and Giuseppe too. Whether Jacques lived or died, the manuscript had to be retrieved.

It was eerie going through the gate of Vatican City again. Dancey showed his identification card, and when the guard looked at it, he half expected sirens to go off, a platoon of Swiss guards in their Michelangelo tights to come jogging down the street, petards on the hoist, and hustle him off to the Holy Father himself, who would assign him some dreadful penance and confine him in partibus infidelium forever. But he was just waved through. He walked on rubbery legs past the post office and on to the courtyard that provided parking for the library. The man in the glass cage would surely jerk into animated frenzy when he saw Dancey. He did not. He was not Guido.

"I must see Monsignor Nerone," Dancey told him.

"The prefect! Do you have an appointment?"

"He is expecting me."

"Your name?"

Dancey handed him his identification card. The man picked up a phone, and guarding it with his hand and frowning Dancey away from the little aperture in the glass, he rang, Dancey presumed, Nerone's office. The conversation was not brief. In the midst of it, the man asked for Dancey's identification card, discovered he already had it, compared it and the visitor's face several times, handed back the card, and listened. Finally he hung up, rose and came out of his cage.

"This way, please."

"Where is Guido?"

"You knew him!" The man's eyes suggested a goiter.

"Slightly."

"God rest his soul."

"I hadn't heard."

Were there still others he had not heard of? Guido's replacement led Dancey into the corridor where Strommer's office had been. The door was closed. They went by it. The man had leather heels, which made a resounding noise on the marble floor, great squares of black and white, a checkerboard with Nerone's office at the end of the hall in the king's position. The guard came to a semblance of attention at the door and indicated that Dancey should enter.

Seated behind a desk was a white-haired prelate, quite old, as old as Jacques. He got to his feet slowly, one hand on his scarlet skullcap. Once on his feet, he tugged his sash up over his massive stomach, getting it armpit high. Standing had not added much more than a cubit to his stature. He peered at Dancey over half glasses.

"I wish to see Monsignor Nerone," Dancey said.

"Yes?"

"Roberto Nerone."

"I am Monsignor Roberto Nerone," he said patiently. "I am the prefect of the Biblioteca Apostolica Vaticana."

Inventiveness returned, bobbing to the surface of his confusion like a cork.

"I bring you greetings from Father Edward Synan, Monsignor."

"Ah." His smile showed only his lower teeth, which represented a fortune in dentistry and, Dancey supposed, a plenary indulgence in pain as well. "You are from Toronto?"

"No. Washington."

"Then you will know my good friend Dean Jude Dougherty."

Dancey took the offered chair. He spent fifteen minutes with him, exchanging chitchat of a sort to interest only medievalists. Nerone was upset that Dancey did not seem to know Astrik Gabriel. When Dancey excused himself, the monsignor said that he hoped Dancey would have a profitable visit working in the Vatican Library, and if he could be of any assistance, Dancey need only call on him. Was he quite sure he did not know Canon

Gabriel? Dancey thanked the prefect with extreme unction, backing out of the office, then turned and moved quickly over the
checkerboard and into the outside world and some very badly
needed fresh air.

20

There were several cars in the street outside Polly's apartment that might have been hers, one Fiat being very much like another. Dancey waved at the *portiera* with his free hand when he crossed the lobby; he had the dress box under his other arm. The *portiera* scrambled to her feet, and Dancey tried to ignore her jabbering, but before he could get the elevator door closed, she placed her sizable foot inside and told him he could not go upstairs while the *signora* was out.

"She is in."

"No *signore*. She is not. I saw her leave with my own two eyes." She put her fingers under the organs named and pulled down the lower lids, exposing inflamed underflesh.

"You must have been mistaken."

She was enraged by the suggestion that anything could happen in this building without her knowledge. She insisted that the *signorina* had left half an hour before. It was all Dancey could do to keep his patience. The day had been one of dizzying reversals. One by one, he had been deprived of people he could trust. He was wholly bereft of help and he had returned to Polly's as to the only port in a storm of confusion. And now this hag of a *portiera* refused him entry. Reason being out of the question, he resorted to cunning. Smiling sweetly, agreeing entirely, he left the building and started up the street.

Five minutes later, he entered the tobacco shop across the street from Polly's. He bought a packet of cigarettes, opened it, offered the clerk one, then loitered near the doorway, smoking, looking speculatively at the magazines, his eyes on Polly's building.

He had no idea when she might return and hoped that he would not have to wait until she did. The *portiera* came outside with her broom. Off on a flight? She stood for a moment surveying in a proprietary way the small domain represented by the sidewalk in front of the building. Empires come in all sizes. She began to sweep, moving the broom briskly back and forth, progressing away from the entrance, her back to Dancey. He left the tobacco store, darted across the street and into the building unnoticed. He took the stairs and arrived on the top floor winded. The key was in its hiding place, under the flowerpot in the hallway. Dancey put it back there after he had unlocked the door.

Despite the hour of day, the apartment was cool. He dropped the dress box on a chair and noticed that the shoulder bag he had brought from the hotel was on the floor, between the bed and the wall. He unzipped it and rummaged through Mrs. Parson's clothes, almost surprised to find them still there. And the wig. He untied the box and stuffed the lire into the shoulder bag.

The bed tempted him briefly, but memories of last night told against it, as if it promised weariness as much as rest. He smiled. Dear Polly. He went out onto the balcony and collapsed in a wicker chair. Sun slanted down on him, but there was a slight compensatory breeze. Closing his eyes, he listened to the roar of traffic, horns, brakes, voices. The silence of the apartment seemed audible too. At the moment he did not want to think of a thing. He made of his mind a total blank. There was no reason not to sleep if sleep came. It came.

He dreamed that Polly came home and they talked and the events of the past twenty-four hours became intelligible by proving not to have happened at all. Giuseppe was alive and well, speeding obsequiously along the corridors of the Columbus Hotel. Dancey's first run with a manuscript had gone off without a hitch, and when Jacques discovered what was going on, he approved of it, so long as James Dancey was in charge. Strommer, puffing, pudgy Strommer, was destined to die in his bed many years hence and his bed would be in the Horatian villa he dreamed of. Cielli was everything an American businessman abroad should be and Lancia's office phoned to say that the results of Dancey's physical were so impressive that they would like permission to publish them in a medical journal. Polly shyly confessed that Dancey had spoiled her for other men. He was smiling when he came awake to the ringing of the telephone. The darkness surprised him, as if the sun had gone off like a bulb.

He heaved himself from the chair before he was completely sure where he was. The balcony ledge was belt high and contact with it, together with the sudden view of the street four floors below, snapped him awake. But he was yawning abundantly when he picked up the phone and put it to his ear.

"Mmmm?" Dancey nearly gagged trying to get his mouth closed—*oscitatio interrupta*—and when he did, tried to make this sexless hum serve as an answer.

"Polly, is that you?"

Dancey put down the phone. Cielli's voice had dissipated the euphoria that had accompanied his dream. Had he just now heard a thief and murderer? And why would Cielli call Polly?

The apartment no longer seemed a haven. Dancey went back onto the balcony, and, looking down, saw Polly wedging her car into a parking space. He relaxed. It was suddenly impossible to think of that foreshortened figure as an object of distrust. Was it her fault that Cielli telephoned her? The sound of her slamming car door rose to him. She stood on the driver's side of the car, illumined by passing headlights, waiting for a break in traffic, and when it came, she crossed the street. Thinking that she might not be coming up, Dancey cupped his hands to his mouth.

"Polly!"

But his voice did not carry from this height with the traffic as competition. Polly had reached the opposite side of the street and stopped at a doorway, in which Dancey now noticed a large figure. The man stepped onto the walk and into the light. It was Bruno, Dancey's pursuer, the man with whom Nathaniel Gainer had been on such friendly terms. It was clear that Polly found him equally familiar. She had to look up when she talked to him. Dancey stepped back, as if she might see him on the balcony, but she was completely absorbed. He could not read the meaning of her expression.

Polly touched the man's arm and turned toward the street. She did look up to the balcony then and Dancey went hurriedly inside. He continued to the door and let himself out.

He had noticed that although Polly's apartment was on the top floor, the stairs continued. He mounted them now and they brought him to a door which admitted him, as he had hoped it would, to the roof of the building. And one roof led to another, stretching and curving away. He could almost imagine traversing Rome by way of its rooftops. But all he really needed was to get far enough away to evade the stolid Bruno, lolling in the doorway.

From the rooftop, the Pincio was visible above him, looking like a hanging garden in the moonlight. There was a sort of potting shed on the roof of Polly's building, and odds and ends of maintenance lay about, courtesy of the *portiera's* husband, presumably. Dancey stepped over a low tarred ledge onto the neighboring building, where an effort had been made to provide a sunning area for the tenants. This gave him confidence since, though it was in shadow, there was less chance of barking a shin, and he quickened his pace. And tripped over something. Someone. A body. Two bodies. There was an angry male grunt and a woman's voice asked, "What is it?" Dancey scrambled to his feet, using the couple to do so, discovering in the process that they were coupled indeed. Doubtless the magic went out of things for them then.

"What the hell are you doing?" the man's voice whispered hoarsely. He seemed to be speaking into Dancey's very ear.

His impaled beloved took this question to be directed at her and with a heave of her hips she spilled him into deeper darkness. Groping, Dancey edged away from them. His confidence in his sense of direction had been shaken by that uncleared hurdle on his path. Behind him the lovers' quarrel gathered momentum and he bumped into the superstructure containing the door giving admission to the building. The presence of that matey couple suggested the door was unlocked and he might take these stairs, but their rising voices prodded him onward.

He skipped onto the next roof and, hands extended before him like a sleepwalker, moved at a steady pace. There were no further incidents until he reached a roof where a dog was penned. His wailing warning bark propelled Dancey on his way. He was desperate now to get off the rooftops. If that couple ever resolved their differences, it might occur to them to alert the police about the stealthy intruder gliding over the rooftops. His problem now was that the stairway doors he tried were locked. Even a moderately security-conscious *portiere* would, he recognized, see to it that a sturdy lock was put on such a door. His plan of escape was looking progressively less inspired, but he had little choice except to keep moving on to the next roof. Eventually, this too was foreclosed. A cross street intervened and, looking over the ledge, he saw the street below. He also saw the fire escape ladder embedded in the wall, leading to an iron outside stairway.

He was over the ledge in a moment and going hand under hand down the ladder. The first grilled landing of the fire escape bonged when he dropped onto it. He started down the stairs and then stopped dead. On the landing below, a mattress had been laid out and there was a body on it. Apparently only one, but after his experience on the rooftop, Dancey looked closely to make sure. One. It was a man, thin, bald, apparently quite old. He was reminiscent of the sleeping figure preserved in lava at Pompeii. Dancey crept down step by step until the next step he took would have to be onto the mattress. The man's breathing was rough and regular, not quite a snore. Dancey put his foot on the surface of the mattress, but did not at first exert his full weight. Slowly, slowly, he let his foot sink in. As it did, the sleeping man began to roll into the indentation thus created. His breathing did not alter, though it became less audible. Now all Dancey's weight was on the one foot and the man's side was snug against his ankle. He stepped over him with his free foot and then, again slowly, extracted the first. The man returned to his original position. The sound of his breathing stopped. So did Dancey's. Suddenly the man began to gasp, several quick intakes of air. Dancey's flesh tingled with fear. He was poised over the old man like the god Mercury, one foot planted, the other aloft, as if immobilized in flight. Say it with flowers. His unnerving inhalations done, the old man emitted a sighing sough and subsided into a regular pulmonary rhythm again. Dancey continued the step he had begun centuries before— forever he pursues and she is pursued—and went rapidly down the fire escape. It brought him to street level and eye to eye with a man in a black turtleneck sweater who was holding a gun.

21

The man got one hand in Dancey's armpit, laid the gun alongside his cheek, and propelled him swiftly up the street. Dancey's legs seemed to have developed several extra joints, but they were remarkably responsive to the urgings of his captor. The sight of the black turtleneck sweater, the menace of the gun, brought back the sheer terror with which he had lain beneath the customs table at Fiumicino. The fact that the gun had not yet gone off was small consolation, since they seemed to be speeding toward some less public place of execution. Dancey tried to convey to his feet the sense of self-preservation. If he could not plant them, he could at least get them to drag, slowing down their progress.

Around the corner of the building came another man, also in black turtleneck, also carrying a gun. Hope left Dancey as audibly as a sigh. He had been all but helpless against one of them. Against a squad he had no chance at all. The second man got his hand into Dancey's other armpit, he was raised from the sidewalk and literally carried around the corner of the building.

Behind the wheel of a Fiat sports car, its top down, lounged Monsignor Roberto Nerone. Dancey's progress ended beside the car, the two black turtlenecks flanking him like acolytes. Nerone was not in clerical clothes. He wore a blazer and a turtleneck. Black. His expression was at once triumphant and dour. A report was given of Dancey's descent and capture.

"Very enterprising, Dr. Dancey. Get into the car."

"What are you doing here?"

"Catching a thief. We had covered every possible exit. It was only a matter of time."

"We?" Dancey looked at the men beside him. "Ottobre Quindici?"

The grip on both his arms tightened. Nerone gave an order and Dancey was hustled around the car and shoved in beside Nerone.

"I know you're not Monsignor Nerone," Dancey said, "You're a fake."

"A more persuasive one than I had hoped. But I am glad the charade is over." His jaw flexed and suddenly his arm moved and the back of his hand smashed into Dancey's face. "Where is the manuscript?"

"I don't have it." Dancey spoke through fireworks. His nose felt broken. He reached for his handkerchief and was immediately pinned to the seat by the two men standing beside the car.

"My nose is bleeding."

"So it is. Where is the manuscript, Dancey?"

"You know I don't have it. I have been chased all over Rome. I am being hunted by the police."

"Because you are a thief."

"And what are you? Who are you?"

"My name is Carlo Posti. As to what I am, I would prefer that I not have to show you. Why did you kill Giuseppe?"

"I didn't kill Giuseppe!"

Again he was struck in the face. Dancey cried out, looking wildly around. Was it possible that he could be treated like this on a public street without anyone taking notice? Before he had been struck a second time, he was prepared to tell the bogus Nerone, Carlo Posti, what he knew, but with the renewal of pain, the stubbornness that had sustained him thus far surged up in him. Blood was running freely from his nose now. Posti observed the effect of his blows in a clinical manner.

"You have said it, Dancey. We are Ottobre Quindici. Do not count on restraint or sympathy. Remember your experience at the airport. There are no limits for us. No limits at all. You understand?

Good. Tell me precisely what happened when you brought the manuscript to the hotel."

Posti leaned toward him. He might have been his persona again, Monsignor Nerone, anxious for precision and detail. Dancey looked at the man. How had he ever taken him for a monsignor, a priest, a human being? At that moment, Dancey was certain that he could withstand anything before he would say a word to this monster. But then, after a nod from Posti, a man beside the car pulled Dancey's arm up behind his back and the excruciating pain began. His cry was involuntary. Posti struck him again. Dancey's mouth was full of blood and he began to choke.

The car motor started and almost immediately they began to move. Dancey was thrown back against the seat and his head snapped back. He stared up at the sky, visible beyond the tops of buildings; he got his handkerchief out and brought it gingerly to his nose. Breathing through his mouth, feeling the pain dull, or perhaps simply become familiar, he glanced at Posti, who was driving with the manic concentration of the Roman motorist. His actor's profile was impassive. No one would have guessed that he had just savaged his passenger. Dancey straightened in the seat, seeking a minimum of discomfort. Posti cut into the Corso, where traffic was dense, and visibly relaxed when his Fiat blended in with all the others.

"Now then, Dr. Dancey."

"It was all a fake," Dancey said. "I know that now. There was no microfiche project. There was no studio. All you wanted was one manuscript." Dancey's try at a laugh was pitiful. Posti glanced at him. "The one thing you wanted you didn't get."

"It is no good to you, Dancey. You cannot sell it. You cannot get out of the country with it."

"Neither can you."

"Selling it or smuggling it is not in our plans. Nor injuring it. Where did you put it?"

"Look, Posti, or whatever the hell your name is..." Dancey paused. "The Trattoria Posti," he said musingly.

"Dancey, my friends are following us in another car. This is merely an interlude. If you do not want to suffer more, you will take this opportunity to tell me where the manuscript is. That is all I wish to know. Once you have told me, I will stop the car and you are free to go."

"I'll bet."

"I promise you."

"Nothing could be more precious to me than one of your promises. Your word is your bond. If you assure me—"

Posti's fist slammed into Dancey's stomach, doubling him over. His nose began to bleed freely again.

"You are mistaken if you think silence can protect you, Dancey. As long as you are silent, you are apt to receive blows like that one. Many blows. Now, I ask you. Is it worth all this pain simply to postpone what you must eventually do? Sit up!"

Posti had swung off the Corso and parked. Dancey put his back against the seat. He became aware of the black-turtlenecked duo beside the car. The thought of crueler pain was too much for him.

"Ernesto Cielli has it." He said the words *recto tono*, to diminish his sense of betrayal and weakness.

Carlo Posti's laughter was sparkling and incredulous. "That won't do, Dancey. Now, I ask you again, just once more. Who has the manuscript?"

"Cielli! He tried to sell it to Nathaniel Gainer. I was there when Gainer got the phone call."

Posti was shaking his head, but his eyes hung on Dancey's face and in their depths was the beginning of doubt. Or more than the beginning. Dancey was reminded of Gainer's eyes when he had spoken of Cielli. The men beside the car shuffled impatiently and Posti glanced at them.

"I don't believe you, Dancey." But his voice said otherwise.

"Why should you? Find out for yourself." And then, as if he could make amends for the truth with a lie, he went on: "He has it in his apartment at the castle."

"The castle!" Posti relaxed into disbelief. "Does Cielli live in the Castel Sant' Angelo?"

"It is a Norman castle, on the coast above Ostia. He gave me a

162

key." Dancey plunged his hand into his pocket and immediately his arm was gripped, but Posti indicated that Dancey was to be permitted to show what he had in his pocket. When he had the key out, Posti and the other two stared at it.

"That is the key to the castle?"

"It is the key Cielli gave me. He wanted me to go there, to be safe. He has the manuscript."

A conference ensued. Posti got out of the car and huddled with the other two. Dancey's shoulder was held in a punishing grip while this was going on, the pressure altering with the discussion. He was aware of the fact that they did not believe him. He had introduced a disturbing note into the proceedings. He had told the truth and it did not matter. Was it possible that the Thomistic manuscript would not fall into the hands of Ottobre Quindici even now?

Posti had parked in a narrow street, a few blocks from the Piazza Venezia. Behind them, the noisy hum of the Corso was audible, but here they were in a deserted street that might have dated from the Middle Ages, all its inhabitants long since dust. Dancey, trying to catch the drift of the whispers of his captors, trying to adjust to the realization that the man he had thought was a monsignor from the Vatican Library was a member of Ottobre Quindici, thought of breaking loose and running, but the idea seemed wholly theoretical. "You are perfect for our purposes." Those words, spoken in the Café di Napoli in Washington, had filled him with pride. Now he saw their true meaning. He had been the ideal dupe, the perfect patsy. If the plot to steal a manuscript from the Vatican Library had gone awry, it was no credit to James Dancey.

The conference was over. Posti, behind the wheel again, started the car.

"We will go to the castle, Dancey. God help you if the manuscript is not there. Give me that key."

For answer, Dancey tossed it over his shoulder. It clanged on the cobbles. A moment later it was back, in the hand of one of Posti's turtlenecked aides. Posti put it in his pocket.

"I don't know if the manuscript is at the castle."

163

Posti looked at him. "Were you also lying when you said Cielli has it?"

Posti feinted with his hand, and Dancey's stomach tightened in painful anticipation. "No! That's the truth. Cielli has it."

His tone commanded belief. Whatever lingering doubt Posti had had seemed gone. He turned away, his expression determined, but puzzled too. Posti gunned the car through a deserted piazza, drove down streets that would have been narrow for pedestrians in single file, and emerged on the Via del Teatro di Marcello. They were on the way to Ostia, followed by Dancey's captors in a Fiat sedan.

The roar of the wind, the road to Ostia. Despite the night sky above, he was reminded of driving to the sea with Polly for their picnic on the beach. It was like having memories of some impossibly naïve ancestor, though it had been only days before. Dancey did not want to think large thoughts. He did not understand the events in which he had been caught up. He did not want to understand them. He wanted out. He wanted to regain the wonderful insouciance that had been his that afternoon at the beach with Polly. He wanted Polly.

His throat thickened with desire for her. The only comfort he could find in his present impossible situation was that he had drawn these monsters away from Polly's apartment. Thank God he had left. He did not understand what she had been saying to Bruno. Bruno, whatever else might be said of him, was not a terrorist, not a thief, not a killer. Apparently he was a cop. Where was he now when Dancey needed him?

A road traveled twice is shorter. Soon, too soon, the lights of Ostia were visible. "North?" Posti asked. Dancey nodded. Posti signaled to the sedan and made the turn. He had been moving at a good clip before turning onto the coastal road, but now he put the accelerator to the floor. Dancey watched the needle pass 100 kilometers and continue moving. The shadowy countryside swept by and the roar of the wind was deafening. Dancey, looking over his shoulder, his hair whipping on his head, could not make out the sedan. There was only a blur of headlights following them.

After several miles of breakneck speed, Posti flicked off the headlights and they hurtled onward into comparative darkness. Dancey nearly lifted from his seat with terror. But the road was dimly visible still. Posti began to slow then, but he was still going fast when he turned off the road, to the right, away from the sea. He made a crunching, complaining U-turn on gravel, stones spitting into the night, and came to a stop facing the highway.

"I will confront Cielli alone," Posti said. He spoke aloud, but it was himself he addressed. Fishing a gun from inside his blazer, he looked at Dancey. "You and I."

They remained there five minutes. Several dozen cars went past on the road, among them, presumably, Posti's cohorts from Ottobre Quindici. When they pulled onto the highway again, it was only a matter of three or four miles before they came to the castle road. Posti turned off his lights again when he left the highway, a practice that was no less unnerving the second time. When he switched on the headlights again, Dancey could see ahead, silhouetted against the sky, the great notched hulk of the Norman castle.

They followed the road past the church, where according to Polly, fashionable weddings were held, dipped down between the rows of houses and came to a stop in the shadow of the castle. Motor off. Silence. From somewhere came the thin strains of a popular ballad, madly anachronistic, an abrasive encounter of the 11th and 20th centuries. Polly had said there were several apartments in the renovated castle and the music suggested a radio or television, ordinary people, the proximity of the normal. Posti's gun, pointed at Dancey, canceled all that.

They got out of the car. There was a moment when Dancey thought of making a break, just running off into the darkness, heading for the beach, for help. But who could help him now? The futility of flight pressed upon him like the darkness itself. He accompanied Carlo Posti across a wooden bridge like a lamb to the slaughter and they came into the great echoing entry hall of the castle.

Despite the dimensions of the hall, Posti seemed oppressed by the confinement of its walls, as if he needed the whole of night in which to operate. The setting impressed itself on Dancey, a last meal for his eyes. A door opened, the popular tune crescendoed, and a woman looked out in momentary expectancy before disappointment came. Posti, his gun concealed, was instantly the suave impostor of the Italian Embassy in Washington. He told the woman they had come to see Signor Cielli. His manner won her, but it was somewhat petulantly that she gave them directions. She pulled her door closed, and the ballad and the wedge of light she had admitted to the hall disappeared with her.

They went along a passage and found the stairway the woman had mentioned, winding stone steps up which Dancey climbed, prodded by Posti's gun. At the top of the stairs, they came to what seemed an opening in the wall. Through it Dancey saw a gangway like a suspended bridge extending to the towerlike portion of the castle. On the opposite side was a door and beside it a small window, brightly lit. There was a potted geranium on the window sill. Fairyland. The gangway had to be negotiated one at a time. When Dancey, urged on by the muzzle of Posti's gun, stepped onto it, it began to sway, and he grasped the railings. He hesitated, but behind him Posti ordered him to move. Dancey advanced to the middle of the swaying bridge and stopped. He was as much outdoors as in. He could hear the murmur of the sea, the grinding sound of crickets and, from far off, the hum of traffic. The sky was visible above him, fleecy clouds, pale against an inky background, and far far off, stars, planets, elsewhere. The Neoplatonists taught that after death the soul commences a long astral journey, moving ever outward, from star to star, being purged of its earthly attachments as it ascends. Dancey was very conscious of his earthly attachments.

"Keep moving," Posti commanded.

A new sound added itself to those of the night. A car. Lights raked the walls of the castle, there was a squeal of brakes and the sound of sliding on gravel. A horn began to blast. Dancey was aware of Posti coming up behind him and then the door at the end of the gangway opened and Ernesto Cielli appeared, blinking against the dark. Posti's hand extended past Dancey's face, holding the gun.

"Dancey?" Cielli said, recognizing him, and there was a smile of welcome on his treacherous face.

Dancey kicked backward, catching Posti on the shin, spun around, pushing his arm away. There was the roar of the gun going off. The sound enraged Dancey and he levered Posti over his leg and pushed him toward Cielli, who, however startled he must have been by the gunshot, had advanced onto the swaying gangway.

"Posti," he growled, grabbing the man when Dancey shoved him. Cielli twisted the younger man and bent him over the railing. There was the sound of the gun clattering somewhere far below. Dancey got the hell off the gangway, got inside and went slipping and sliding down the stone steps. He loped along the corridor, past the open door that framed the startled woman, who yet seemed to sway with the tempo of her music.

He was outside when he heard the cry. Posti. A great shout of despair, rage, terror. Posti had followed his gun over the railing and into the silence below. Dancey crossed the moat on the run and a moment later was in the crushing grip of Bruno, who popped nimbly from the car that had pulled up behind Posti's.

Dancey struggled wildly in the gorilla's arms, crying out with rage. He had not escaped Posti and Ottobre Quindici to be arrested and rot in a Naples jail for a crime he had not committed. And then, as it might be an angel's, he heard Polly's voice.

"Jimmy, for heaven's sake, get into the car."

Bruno released him. Dancey got into the car, beside Polly. Bruno got in back. And moments later they were roaring away from the castle, passing as they went a Fiat sedan groping its way down the road to the castle.

22

Polly crouched over the wheel, intent on her Grand Prix driving, while behind, wedged into the diminutive back seat, Bruno acted as tail gunner. Knees driven up beneath his chin, holding a gun that went well with his meaty, oversized hand, he looked back at the disappearing taillights of the Fiat sedan.

"They're Ottobre Quindici," Dancey cried, immediately regretting his breathless tone. He repeated this to Polly in what he hoped was a more offhand manner. She ignored him.

She had reached the coastal highway now and whatever restraints had been imposed on her lust for speed by the winding road leading from the castle were removed. Again the roar of the wind and a warm night turned cool by speed. In the circumstances, Dancey found Polly's suicidal style of driving almost soothing. With every added kilometer he was getting farther and farther away from the feel of Carlo Posti's gun, prodding, prodding, and from the awful swaying gangway that led to Cielli's Grimm Brothers door. He thought he would remember forever Cielli opening the door and smiling in welcome to Dancey, imperfectly perceived in the night. Had he thought Dancey was belatedly taking him up on his offer to spirit him out of the country? Now Dancey had the mordant certainty that his departure would have been like that of Carlo Posti.

Death by falling. The thought added a deeper chill to that of the whipped-up night air, and Dancey shivered. His legs ached like arrangements of charley horses, and though his nose had stopped

169

bleeding, he felt that at any moment he would be asked to say a few words of thanks to his trainer, congratulate his opponent and say Hi to mom before crawling from the ring. His nose did not seem broken when he ran a tentative finger along it. Polly became aware of these explorations. She laid her hand on his thigh.

"You only love my body," Dancey whispered.

Her brow knitted. She smiled. "Can't hear you," she shouted.

"I'm not in the mood." Dancey smiled back. "Do you think I'm a machine? Do you think I have no feelings?"

Polly slowed down and leaned an ear toward him. "What?"

"Don't slow down," Bruno yelped behind them. Dancey turned and the huge man looked reprovingly at him. "You're not out of the woods yet."

"Who are you?"

Bruno ignored him. Polly ignored him. Having negotiated Ostia, she now had before her the vast four-lane limited-access road to Rome, and any remnant of prudence she possessed deserted her. She settled back in her seat, only her fingertips touching the wheel, from beneath, holding it as might a disdainful Atlas. It was possible to believe that there was no gas pedal at all intervening between her shoe and the floorboards. On her lips there was a sensuous smile. Oh, there was no doubt of it. Dancey had a rival. This car. Speed. He put a hand on her leg and she covered it with her own.

"I love it," she cried, addressing the universe.

"And that's only my left hand."

"What?"

It was Bruno's gun that prodded Dancey now. "Shut up and let her drive," Bruno said. "And keep your hands to home."

Bruno dispensed demerits primly. Getting Dancey's attention by means of the gun barrel had been a lapse; the big man tucked the weapon away and looked apologetic.

"Is it loaded?"

There went a beautiful friendship. Bruno wrote him off as a nut. Dancey was in a state of shock. The horror and confusions of the past twenty-four hours, the cumulative effect of his several flights, physical punishment, the emotional roller coaster he had been on—all these suddenly immobilized him. The impulse to laugh gave way to the fear that the wind would suck him out of the car, that he was imperfectly anchored in the world. He gripped the edges of his seat. He looked jerkily to left and right. Where was the seat belt? He wanted to be strapped in. If he was not strapped in immediately, he was in danger of being blown from the car.

Bruno's hand descended on his shoulder. "I'll hold you down. Don't worry."

Apparently he had voiced his fear. "Harder."

Bruno pressed down harder, using both hands now. Polly looked at Dancey with alarm. He smiled reassurance. There was no need for her to panic just because he was lighter than air. Air. Wind. It was music in his ears, conveying something to the seashell of his whorled ear. He canted his head, trying to pick up the message. From a distance, he heard Polly speaking. Then Bruno. They seemed to agree on something. A sharp sensation on the side of his neck. Dancey relaxed.

"Did you hurt him?"

"Never fear."

Later they woke him up to give him a sleeping pill. Well, a sedative. He was in bed. Lancia was there. The fact that the needle he held did not induce terror suggested that he had already used it.

"To make you sleep, Jimmy," Polly said, an ectoplasmic presence. "You need rest."

"Not in your apartment."

"You're at the hotel. In your room."

"I meant you."

"She's spending the night with me," Nathaniel Gainer said.

Dancey wanted to ask Lancia if he would inform his regular patients where he had moved his office, but his voice was no longer taking messages from his brain. Bruno. Gainer. Lancia. Why did he feel so safe and sound, surrounded by his enemies? Except Polly, of course. Polly was his friend. He took the thought of her into the dark and did dark things with her.

23

His room in the Columbus Hotel was not a reassuring place in which to wake up. The doors of the balcony were open and the sun seemed high; lazy, summery, soporific sounds lifted from outside; on the ceiling little secondhand suns shimmered and moved nervously about, glancing from some watery surface outside. Sounds, colors, lines, planes, smells, the feel of sheet on leg and chest and arm—these were elements of a world Dancey could not quite reconstruct. He did not want to reconstruct it. He preferred an atomized, fragmented experience that did not accommodate the questions that gathered in the room.

The transition from sense data to things was effected by remembering Giuseppe. Dancey's eyes flew to the door and he had a vivid image of the porter's head thrusting into the room. The bed he lay on had been the temporary repository of the Thomistic autograph.

Dancey leaped out of bed. For a mad moment, he hoped that by tearing back the sheets he would reveal the package Strommer had given him, and the fat librarian and a cast of thousands would converge on him, crying, "Surprise, surprise. April fool." But beneath the sheet was a mattress. Beneath the mattress was a box spring. And beneath the bed was the floor, and so on down to the ultimate turtle sustaining it all. He did not get to choose his surprises.

Shaved and showered, he dressed in clean, dry clothes taken from his suitcase. Was he alone? He did not want to go out onto the balcony for fear the redoubtable Mrs. Parson might be on hers, but from what he could see of the courtyard, it looked peaceful and deserted. The telephone. Should he call room service and order breakfast? But the thought of eating in that room did not appeal. The thought of remaining in the Columbus Hotel did not appeal. Dancey went to the door, eased it open and looked out. At the end of the hall, by the elevator, Bruno sat in a straight-back chair. His eyes were closed. Asleep on the job? Ten demerits.

Out in the hallway, Dancey closed his door without engaging the lock and tiptoed in the opposite direction, toward the stone stairway he had taken with Giuseppe. He did not look back. There was no one on the stairs. On the first floor, he could not resist a glance at the door of Giuseppe's room. Dear God. Then it was outside, across the courtyard, through the garage and into the Borgo Santo Spirito.

Dancey took a table at an outdoor café and ordered cappuccino, thereby reminding himself of that first day with Polly. Memories of Polly were pleasant; let them come. In Gainer's apartment. On the beach. Polly trying on Mrs. Parson's wig. Polly crossing a street in defiance of instant death and with equal defiance showing her finger to the world. Dear Polly, antic, sexy, obsessed with God. Dancey smiled, as if he knew what was going on. Is this how it is with the retarded, never quite sure of the meaning of events, hanging on to close, real certainties, leaving metaphysics and sweeping theories to their betters?

Across the street, two kids were playing with a soccer ball. Dancey watched them, amazed at what they could do with the ball using only their feet. One of them stood against the wall, playing goalie, while the other approached, guiding the ball with his foot, intent on faking out the goalie by drawing him to the right until, lightning quick, the ball sailed through the air. The goalie was as agile as his adversary, but finally he missed one and the victor danced around in the street, hands raised high above his head. At another table, someone began to clap and the kid stopped celebrating. He looked resentfully at his solitary fan, clearly not welcoming the real world to the realm of his fantasy.

174

No more did Dancey feel part of the real world. He finished his coffee and stood. There was only one person he wanted to see and he decided to go on foot. He did not like to think how many miles he had traveled on foot since coming to Rome, but vehicular travel had not been more soothing. Reunion with his luggage had enabled him to get into a pair of his own shoes, but the improvement was slight: an old whine in new booties.

"You are not a soccer fan?"

It was the lone applauder. He fell into step with Dancey, who slowed but did not stop. The man's English had an American accent but nonetheless, perhaps because of his lisp, it sounded to Dancey like a learned language. Blond, thin straight nose, blue eyes, slightly shorter than Dancey. A male prostitute, was Dancey's guess.

"Bug off," he said.

"I think you have need of me."

"And I think you flatter yourself."

A radiant smile. "If this were a less public place, I could show you my credentials."

"I should think you'd be more interested in mine."

"But I know that you are Dr. Dancey."

Dancey stopped. What the hell was this? The man's tapered fingers on Dancey's elbow urged him to keep walking. Dancey anchored himself to the pavement. All he needed after what he had been through was a pushy queer. At the moment, the fine-boned Nordic seemed to sum up the decline of the West.

"How would you like it if I called a cop?"

The man's smile, it seemed to Dancey, was joyless, meant not for him but for others, an audience, anyone else. "I am a cop, in a manner of speaking. Please let us continue walking." His fragile-looking fingers produced a steely grip. They walked. A cop? Dancey would not have wanted to get caught alone in an elevator or washroom with this one.

"Show me your ID," Dancey said.

"I'm a thee eye amen."

"What?"

Ahead of them on the sidewalk, a uniformed policeman was taking a respite from directing traffic on the Via della Conciliazione. Dancey had no desire to attract the attention of the uniformed constabulary. Perhaps he was already under arrest. They passed the cop.

"What's the charge?"

"Oh, it's free." An effete smile.

Oh, boy. American police stories had arrived on Italian television and here, it seemed, was the pathetic result. Snappy repartee from the arresting officer, a fey disguise for the tough guy within, irony.

"Where are we going?" They were headed up the Via della Conciliazione toward the Vatican, toward the front of the Columbus Hotel. "Returning to the scene of the crime?"

"Ho ho," the man said mirthlessly. "I must have a long talk with you, Dr. Dancey."

"Am I arrested?"

"No, you're moving."

"When do you get your own show?"

"Behind this jolly façade . . . "

"Not to say gay."

"You're supposed to be the straight man."

"Count on it."

His name was Horne and he was a CIA man—it was this that he had lisped earlier—and Dancey did not know if he found the fact incredible or not. Horne's credentials identified him as cultural attaché at the American consulate. All the man's banter was gone when they entered St. Peter's and strolled very slowly toward the main altar. They took an elevator to the roof and continued talking as they walked behind the incredibly huge statues of the apostles that overlook the square. Horne paused and looked up.

"Have you ever been to the top of the dome, Dancey?"

"When I was a kid."

"I've never done it. I started up once, but the narrow staircase gave me claustrophobia."

Horne turned and walked off toward a corner of the roof they were on. There were shops selling religious articles and there were tourists everywhere, their cameras clicking incessantly. How Dancey envied them their carefree vacation. Horne refused a cigarette. "Not in church. Or on it." He smiled, no longer epicene. "So. Where are we now? Do you understand the situation?"

"I feel like the postman."

"More like the letter, actually."

Horne had explained to Dancey that while he had been unconscious in Lancia's office, the doctor had embedded a microdot beneath his skin. There was no need for Dancey to know what was on the microdot, Horne thought, so long as Dancey realized that it was considered most important by several conflicting interests.

"And it puts you in a state of maximum danger."

"That'll be different. Do you know what's on the midrodot?"

"Up to a point, yes."

"Why not tell me? Up to a point."

Horne hummed a few bars of some lesser national anthem. "You have become acquainted with Ottobre Quindici, I believe."

"The terrorists? They nearly shot my ass off."

Horne frowned. "Porres was entitled to our protection. He was betrayed. We shall avenge him."

"Horne, I am a scholar. I have been mixed up enough already."

"Needless to say, our Israeli friends are interested. They are the only ones left with balls. They are concerned, not without reason, that any terrorist group will be co-opted by the Arabs."

"I'm not interested in politics. Do you realize that I voted for Nixon?"

This was true. Dancey, fed up with the mandatory irrational liberalism of the campus, had gone out and voted Four More Years. Like the Thousand Year Reich, this proved to be a briefer thing.

"He'll be vindicated," Horne said enigmatically.

Dancey was conscious of his skin, of the borders of his body. What subdermal hiding place had been selected for the tattletale

177

microdot? He had certainly given Lancia ample opportunity to do his work, though his fainting must have been reinforced by an anesthetic.

"If you want the microdot, have Lancia remove it."

"No."

Did Horne propose to do it himself? Dancey's doubts about the man returned. He dropped his cigarette and ground it beneath his heel, activating a dormant blister. Two nuns went by, their head-dresses billowing like spinnakers. Dancey was for civilization against terrorism; he was not averse to doing his part to avenge Porres. But there were some things he would not do, not even to prevent the further decline of the West. Perhaps if the West had declined more, it would have declined less.

"Nicely put," Horne said approvingly. "It is well that you have retained your sense of humor through these baffling and danger-ous events. Dancey, I am authorized to ask a rather risky favor of you. And not what you're thinking. Please believe that my manner is a disguise, nothing more. Come, let us stroll."

As they walked back and forth beneath the huge sandaled feet of the apostles, the porous marble toes made Dancey conscious of the pain in his own pedal extremities. They wove among the smiling, gawking camera-clicking tourists, a polyglot chorus of exaltation, and Horne's voice, fruity but matter-of-fact, might have been emerging from a far darker dimension of existence than that which contained these gaggling sightseers.

"It is, from our point of view, an inconvenience that the incrimi-nating evidence embedded in you has become entwined with the theft of a rarity from the Vatican Library. Nonetheless, this has happened. The Vatican document—you will have a far better idea than I what it is and how valuable it is—has become a pawn in the game of intelligence."

Horne sighed. The folly of mankind weighed heavily upon him. His summary of events was succinct and telegraphic, as if he were paying by the word. It occurred to Dancey that Horne's reports might have to be short, to facilitate encoding. But he resented the banality that the events he had been caught up in acquired in Horne's swift reconstruction of them.

The phony Nerone, Carlo Posti, was a minor transgressor who until quite recently had been content to live off lonely widows and the neuter Teutons and Britons who hung about on Capri. For generations, his family had lived on the periphery of the Vatican, and he had come to know Ulrich Strommer because the librarian was in the habit of dining in the trattoria operated by Posti's uncle. When the contemplated microfiche project had been canceled, it canceled a plan that Posti had formulated. Or at least at first it seemed to cancel it. Posti convinced Strommer that they could proceed as if the microfiche plan was actually under way.

"If they found a dumb enough accomplice?"

"How were you to know, Dancey? There are worse faults than being trusting."

"I can't believe that Strommer would have taken part in the theft of a manuscript."

"Quite right. He developed a plan of his own, one that would ride piggyback on Posti's and redirect it. He could countenance the removal of a manuscript from the Vatican on two conditions—that it came into the hands of someone who would appreciate its value and treat it accordingly, and that eventually it would be restored to its rightful owner. Obviously Ottobre Quindici fulfilled neither of those conditions."

"Nathaniel Gainer!"

"Bingo. Strommer asked a pitifully small sum from Gainer. The offer was accepted as much out of sympathy as greed. Gainer intended to return the manuscript to the Vatican within twenty-four hours."

It was Posti's connection with Ottobre Quindici, a radical haven for libertines bent on nihilistic action, that drew the attention of the CIA, NATO intelligence and the Israelis. The CIA had already planted an agent in Ottobre Quindici. Porres was an Israeli agent.

"And your man is Ernesto Cielli?"

Horne nodded sadly. "Yes."

"But he stole the manuscript!"

"Cielli, in Gainer's words, is a sonofabitch. No, he's far more complicated than that. This is a strange life, Dancey, I mean that in which I am engaged. Loyalties are either intense or nonexistent. A man who has loyalty and loses it—well, he is like some men when they lose religious faith. To call Cielli a double agent is too mild. The man is a virtuoso of treachery." Horne made an impatient motion with his hand. "It is a long story."

"Polly Osborne?"

"That makes far too short a story of it. Her rejection is part of it, of course. The microdot was Cielli's idea. He seems to have intended it as a curious sort of insurance policy. On the microdot are photographs of Zar, the Ottobre Quindici leader, and his chief lieutenants, plus other incriminating documents. Cielli quite rightly expected the terrorists to be furious when their plan for a highly publicized theft of a cultural treasure was aborted. His trump would be that he had had the microdot embedded in you."

"Has he told Ottobre Quindici about the microdot?"

"I don't know. Perhaps after the contretemps you were involved in at the castle last night, he has had to do so. In any case, I have managed to get word to them."

"To Ottobre Quindici? What the hell for?"

"I said that I have been authorized to ask a risky favor of you."

"Horne, my only concern is to get back the Vatican manuscript. Once that has been returned, you can remove the damned microdot."

"The two things have become intertwined."

"You know Cielli has the manuscript. Go get it."

"Cielli will be dealt with," Horne said grimly. "Our Italian friends are anxious to lay hands on him, and they shall. We in turn are eager to get hold of Zar. And Zar is now anxious to get his hands on you."

"Thanks to you!"

Horne looked apologetic. Dancey must understand that his chief concern was to lure Zar into the open.

"With me?"

"With you. As you remind me, your concern is the retrieval of the Vatican manuscript. Please understand when I say that my impulse was to keep you unaware of the microdot and to employ you as unwitting bait in order to entrap Zar."

"Thanks a hell of a lot."

"My preference was overridden by my superiors. These are times when we must engage in clandestine operations with clean hands." Horne sighed. "I am ordered to do everything possible to aid the Vatican in its effort to recover its property. To this end, Gainer has agreed to meet Cielli's exorbitant price. You will be the intermediary."

"I hand Cielli Gainer's money and he gives me the manuscript?"

"That's right."

"I'm sure there's more."

"The exchange will take place at the Villa Medici tomorrow. I will inform Zar of the time and place."

"You can't seriously expect me to agree to that."

"I expect even less that you will want to face charges of murder and grand larceny."

"Grand larceny?" Dancey had a fleeting thought of the lire he had stuffed into Mrs. Parson's shoulder bag.

"I admit that is a bland phrase, given the way the Italians regard the theft of something like that Vatican manuscript."

"Horne, there's no reason to involve me. Remove the microdot and lure Zar with that. He doesn't want me."

"So he can destroy the microdot with his little microhammer? Among other considerations, we do not have time."

"I have lots of time."

"Even Lancia would require too much time to locate it."

"It can't be that hard to find."

A microdot, Horne reminded him, is infinitesimal in size. Dancey had a sudden memory of Polly's amorous *tour de monde* of his body. Had she been seeking evidence of an incision?

"Mrs. Osborne is a trusted operative. But she has been acting equally as your friend."

"Aren't there electronic means of finding the microdot?"

181

"There are various ways. Alas, we do not have the equipment here and it would be impractical to bring it in."

"Then take me to it."

"Again, Dancey, time. We do not have enough of it."

"You intend to throw me to the lions."

"I assure you that people for whom your safety is not unimportant have considered every possibility. Including, let me repeat, the single alternative open to you."

"Prosecution?"

"Let us not dwell on depressing possibilities."

Horne's conception of the alternative to depressing possibilities differed considerably from Dancey's own. Cielli was even worse than Gainer thought him and Dancey could not imagine that Cielli contemplated a simple quid pro quo at the Villa Medici. Would not such a practiced double-crosser suspect he was being set up?

"Leave these things to us, Dancey. You are a very improvising young man, you have earned the admiration of all of us, but leave this to the professionals."

They said good-bye on the broad front steps of the great basilica, lost in the throngs of tourists and pilgrims. "Good luck," Horne said before mincing off into the church again. He had reassumed his fey persona when they descended from the roof. The exchange was set for the following day and he would not be seeing Horne before then. Dancey was almost sorry to see him go.

He felt more alone than ever when he hailed a cab and gave the driver Polly's address.

24

The *portiera*, a poor loser, pretended not to see Dancey enter the elevator. Perhaps she did not know for sure whether Polly was in and did not choose to risk being overruled by a tenant. In any case, Dancey rose unmolested to Polly's floor and, receiving no answer to two well-spaced knocks on the door, availed himself of the key hidden beneath the flowerpot in the hallway and entered the apartment.

The bed had not been slept in and he remembered having heard in a haze the night before that Polly was going to Gainer's. Before he could act on his decision to telephone her uncle and ask for Polly, the phone rang.

"Did you talk to Horne?"

"Yes. I just got here."

"I know."

"Is that so?"

She laughed. "Surely Horne told you. You have a little transmitter on you. Bruno monitors it. I just heard from him."

On the balcony, a pigeon strutted as if he too knew something Dancey did not know. "You mean the thing Lancia inserted?"

"So he did tell you. What are your plans?"

They had just changed, if she meant his immediate plans. He said, "You know the plan for tomorrow, of course."

"We have to talk about that. Wait for me there."

"No." He sought a plausible lie but could find none. "I have to go."

"Where?"

He thought about that. "Ask Bruno."

He left ten minutes later, over the rooftops, fueled by anger and resentment, emotions with diffuse as well as concentrated targets. There was a desire to confuse the *portiera*. What goes up must come down? Another law of nature shattered. And might he not confuse the monitoring Bruno too? A glance from the balcony revealed that stolid figure in his favorite doorway across the street. What was the range of reception of whatever device he used? Apparently it explained Bruno's presence in the Piazza Bologna the morning Dancey had coffee with Cielli. And it had brought Bruno and Polly after him when Posti and his cohorts in Ottobre Quindici snatched him away to Ostia. This last inference cast doubt on the value of his route of departure, but there are many ways of sowing confusion, of producing conflict between the technical and the visual. Sighing, Dancey undressed. He would leave the apartment in the garb in which he had first returned to it.

Doubtless a mere taste for gamesmanship would not have enabled Dancey to face the prospect of donning again the clothes in which he had fled the Columbus Hotel. The concentrated target of his anger was Horne. The microdot was a bunch of hooey, permissible perhaps to mislead Zar and Ottobre Quindici, adopting the lie that Cielli must have fashioned for them, but it was unforgivable of Horne to lie to Dancey, turning a subdermal transmitter whose object had been to protect Dancey into a fictive microdot guaranteed to frighten him out of his wits. Well, if James Dancey was to take part in the stratagem to regain the manuscript, entrap Zar and Ottobre Quindici, and administer to Cielli his just deserts, he would do so as a free agent and not as a patsy. Leave the worry to professionals, Horne had said. Ha. Porres had been a professional, and for that matter, so was Cielli. If anyone was going to ensure the safety of James Dancey, it was going to be James Dancey himself.

There were anticipatory pains in his feet, which subsided when he discovered that he could slip into a pair of Polly's sandals, sandals like those he had seen on Franciscans, open toes permitting his to emerge unrestrained, a strap that buckled them securely to his feet. In these he could even run. The bra unlocked its mysteries to him and he got into it without difficulty. Just a trace of lipstick, mwah, then on with the wig and, once more, he marveled at the transformation.

His own clothes went into the shoulder bag. He turned on every light in the apartment, turned on the radio too, loud. Jamming Radio Bruno? Time to go.

Except for the barking dog, his passage across the roofs was uneventful. Had the lovers made up their quarrel? he wondered. Had it become clear to the lady that an intruder in their lust had prompted those unkind words from her naughty night rider? He reached the last roof and, hitching up his skirt, went over the side. Having adjusted things on the first balcony, he continued sedately down. At the second landing, seated in an open window, was the baldheaded man whose dreams Dancey had not completely disturbed a few nights before. The man stared as if at an apparition, but surprise gave way to a gap-toothed smile.

"*Buona sera*," he said musically.

Dancey returned the salutation, his own voice throatily musical, and was about to continue down, for all the world as if he had just greeted an acquaintance on the street, when the old man said something Dancey did not catch.

"Pardon, *signore?*"

The old man nodded Dancey close. Dancey hesitated, then leaned toward the harmless old fellow. A practiced hand shot up his skirt and an obscene suggestion was whispered in his ear. Dancey managed to break free before the old man could nuzzle his nose in Mrs. Parson's falsies. Slapping him was a reflex. The man seemed to like it. His cackle accompanied Dancey to the street. Honestly, the things a girl has to put up with.

But Dancey was more shaken than amused, however much the old man's pass proved the effectiveness of his disguise. He hitched his bag high on his shoulder and swung along the street, keeping the sway of his hips to a minimum, Even so, few of the men he passed failed to make a comment, either audibly or with their eyes. Dancey decided that being a woman was a pain in the ass. A target for slavering idiots, he felt reduced to flesh. Was he himself so continuously in heat as these passers-by? From somewhere beneath his padded bra an incipient feminist spoke up. I have a mind, you bastards. I have a soul. Anyone for chess? Thank God he was a male.

Dozens of eyes followed him through the lobby of the Pensione Venezia when he registered as Signora Fulvia Bruni. One teenager with a bold look boarded the elevator with Dancey and waited for him to press a button. He himself pressed none. As they ascended, the boy examined Dancey with shameless lust.

"You are alone, *signorina?*"

"*Bitte?*"

"*Tedesca?*" The boy was taken aback, but emboldened too. If the redhead did not understand Italian, he could express himself with abandon. He did. Dancey was startled by the details of the scenario sketched by this sex maniac.

"Are you a virgin?" Dancey asked sweetly in Italian.

Instant rage. The boy denied it hotly. Dancey might have accused him of selling his family into slavery. He claimed to have had his first experience at the age of nine.

"And in the three years since?"

His smile reminded Dancey of the one he himself had worn into the blood bank in Washington. The *signorina* was playful? Good. He liked that.

"My husband is playful too."

"Abandon him. He is unworthy of you."

"True. But he has the temper of a madman. Would you believe he brought his rifle to Rome? To protect me." Dancey giggled. The boy edged away. The door opened. Dancey looked out, furtively, as if fearful. He turned back to the boy. "Are you coming?"

"But your husband?"

"I'm not sure the rifle is loaded."

"Later, *signora.* Or better, come to my room."

This scene was terminated by the closing of the elevator door. The boy's eyes brimmed with lust and fear as his face was cut from view.

Inside his room, Dancey pulled off the wig and sailed it across the bed. In a minute he had stripped to his shorts. Lack of clothes

186

makes the man. He felt restored to himself. Reluctantly, he admired the guts of the old man and the teen-aged boy. He himself would never have dared to be so direct in address to a woman. His reaction was no clue to what a woman would feel. Faint heart never won fair lady? Nonetheless, Dancey was sure the majority of women would have screeched for help if trapped in an elevator with that importunate precocious youth.

He spent the rest of the day in bed, exulting in anonymity. That night he called Polly.

"Where are you?" she squealed.

"Doesn't Bruno know?"

"His watchamacallit isn't working. He sat on it. Jimmy, come back here. Or I can come get you."

"No."

"Then take a cab."

"I'll stay here."

"But where is here?"

"I'm going to help get that manuscript back, Polly. That is the only thing I'm interested in."

"And then?"

The question curled in her voice, an audible question mark, reminding him of their intimacies. She was just part of Horne's gang, enjoying the fun of wiring Dancey for sound and tracking him through mortal danger, but surely some of her behavior had been sincere. No one could be that thorough an actress. He imagined having returned the manuscript to the Vatican Library, plopping it on the desk of the real Monsignor Nerone. He emerged into St. Peter's square, mission accomplished. What then? Back to the books? Eventually home to the daily reminder that he did not have a job? Suddenly he felt very lonely.

"I don't know."

"The exchange takes place tomorrow afternoon. The Villa Medici. At two o'clock."

"What about the money?"

"I'll bring it to you there. Jimmy, where are you now? Tell me."

"In a *pensione*. I'm all right."

"Don't you want to come back here?"

"I want to. That isn't the point."

"Isn't it?"

"I'll see you tomorrow," he said, and put down the phone.

It was a good thing he had left the apartment if a few sultry questions affected him so much. He must not forget that Polly had played him for a fool. She found him dashing because of his dot or transmitter or what the hell. What could you make of a girl who was all over you like a mink one minute and the next wanted to talk about God? The sad divorcee, the perky picnic partner, the foxy lover, the poor little rich girl—Polly was too much for him.

He took the thought to bed with him, lying sleepless on the high single bed, which would have been at home in a hospital. Hospital. Salvator Mundi. Père Jacques. Best to keep his mind fixed on the little priest. Dancey could believe that there was some mystical connection between the recovery of the stolen manuscript and Jacques' own recovery. His mind returned to the planned exchange on the following day. Did anyone expect him to survive that encounter? Well, by God, he would. He had survived thus far and had surprised them all. He would surprise them again tomorrow.

Polly was the only one who might recognize him in his disguise as Mrs. Parson.

25

Dancey got up early the next morning, washed but postponed
shaving and, after a brief breakfast eaten standing at the counter of
a café, made his way to the Banco di Roma. Signor Ponzi, the
direttore, looked up with apprehension when Dancey stood in the
doorway of his office.

"*Un'altra volta?*" he cried.

"*Un'ultima volta,*" Dancey corrected.

"All of it?"

"Yes."

"In lire?"

"Why not?"

As before, this cushioned the shock, permitting Ponzi to invent a
rate of exchange less damaging to his patriotism and venality.
Dancey was not clear in his own mind why he wanted this money
with him. He had become attached to it, not so much to its physical
reality as to the thought of it. In some obscure way, it belonged to
him, by compensatory justice. Perhaps it represented a destiny
beyond the recovery of the Vatican manuscript. He had brought
Mrs. Parson's shoulder bag with him and the solid slap of the bag
of money against his hip gave him courage for what lay ahead that
afternoon. Dancey was not reluctant to have the money in lire. Any
attempt to gather such an amount in dollars could conceivably
create an undesirable interest in the transaction. Ponzi, thanks to
the percentage he was skimming, had a vested interest in keeping
Dancey's banking habits confidential. But the *direttore* half rose,

tipping forward, when the contents of Dancey's shoulder bag were revealed as this withdrawal joined the rest of the money. Ponzi's eyes took on an exophthalmic cast.

"*Santa buona polenta*," he cried. "Where are you going with all that money?"

"To where neither rust nor moth consumes nor thief breaks in to steal," Dancey said unctuously, and swept from Ponzi's office.

But if heaven was his destination, he hoped he was on a local train and not a *rapido*. Meanwhile, he was concerned about thieves and killers, if not moths and rust.

When he returned to his *pensione*, the oversexed youth who had accosted him in the elevator the night before lounged in the television room off the lobby. His eyes darted to Dancey and then back to the TV. Seeking whom he might devour? It seemed a portent that Dancey's thoughts should now move in biblical grooves. He only hoped that that libidinous lad was not around when he vacated the premises as Mrs. Parson.

Thanks to Polly's sandals, he figured it would take him less than fifteen minutes to get to the Villa Medici. He wanted the entire cast assembled before he got there; he would arrive at the last moment and, taking advantage of surprise and his disguise, pluck the envelope from Polly, exchange it with Cielli for the Thomistic autograph, and be off and running before anyone knew precisely what had happened. He ran this past his mind's eye through several cigarettes and found no flaw in it. Speed and surprise, these were his allies. It was very far from being dark, but Dancey whistled and waited and tried to get his mind on other things.

As it will in moments of stress, theology beckoned. Dancey recalled his unnerving conversation with Polly that first night when, twisted in adulterous sheets, they had spoken of God. Or Polly had, and he had tried to parry the thrust of her remarks. It is often thought that the contingency and surface absurdity of human affairs tell against the existence of God, as if a deity worthy of the name would run the world with the efficiency of a corner store. Dancey was inclined to feel that the very messiness of the world contains a compelling case for the existence of God, of a wise and

190

tolerant God who did not simply wind us up to fulfill narrowly predestined roles. Among academics, something called the Problem of Evil is belabored as a hindrance to belief, but perhaps the absence of evil would be a greater hindrance, since then there would be no one like James Dancey.

Adversity and embarrassment had brought him to a point Polly had apparently reached before they met. Dancey found it difficult, after his experiences in Rome, to see his life as a rational arrangement of events presided over omnisciently by himself. He seemed, like everyone else, to be the butt of a joke whose point was to teach him to laugh at himself. Chesterton listed a sense of humor among the divine attributes.

Such speculation is possible, or desirable, only in moments of tranquillity, or in such interludes as that in which Dancey then found himself. This makes it no less welcome when its moment comes. So Dancey, wallowing in contemplation, wishing that Polly were there to trade stories with, waited for his watch and the thousand bells of Rome to inch their way to two o'clock.

At one-thirty Dancey leaned toward the mirror to check his cleavage. Running the tip of his tongue across his lips, he made them glisten. He regarded himself with drooping lids. There was no doubt about it: he made one hell of a woman. This would be the last time he got himself up like this. The medievals thought of woman as a failed man. *Dimidium animae meae.* A lovely thought. What wonder then that a man can become so perfect a woman.

The bells rang out the half-hour and he rose. The bag full of lire lay on the bed. He could not leave it here. With a sighing exhalation, he picked it up. The burden of wealth. At the door, he surveyed the room. Would he ever see it again? He decided to take along a pair of trousers and a shirt. A quick change of gender could very well provide just the margin of safety he needed. He felt good when he left.

Complacency stayed with him as he went down in the elevator and did not go until he passed the television room and, out of the corner of his eye, saw his teen-aged tormentor of the night before lift from his chair as if prodded by some irresistible aphrodisiac.

Dancey quickened his step, whirled through the door and started up the street, but he despaired of losing the boy. Such ardor could not be quenched by anything short of an orgy. But Dancey kept his eyes straight ahead when the boy fell into step beside him.

"*Signora*, you are beautiful today," the boy panted. He had to dodge and weave to keep beside Dancey on the busy sidewalk.

"I shall call a policeman."

"A policeman! *Signora*, I will apply at the academy and become a policeman in order to answer your summons."

"Please. I am in a hurry."

"Your impatience is the twin of mine."

Dancey glanced at the kid. His eyes looked feverish, his teeth glistened, he placed a yearning hand on his breast. Apparently he had decided to exchange a poetic approach for the more direct one of the night before.

Dancey stopped and put a confiding hand on the boy's arm. "Can you keep a secret?"

Could he keep a secret? He would tell the world he could.

"Good. Please understand." Dancey paused. "My husband does not."

"Your husband." The boy spat symbolically toward the curb, causing a matron in black to step lively and shake a fist at him.

"I am going to see my lover."

The boy's face contorted. "I will kill him."

"You can't. He's a cripple."

"Then I will kill myself."

Dancey might have agreed to this excellent suggestion if the boy had not grabbed his own throat with both hands and begun to simulate suicide right there on the sidewalk. Dancey was painfully aware that they were creating a scene.

"Stop that. Go back to the *pensione*."

"I will kill myself."

"Watch television."

"I hate television. I never watch it."

Dancey began to walk and the boy hurried along with him. A sense of desperation came over Dancey. This boy was just the unforeseen detail that spelled disaster. He could not arrive at the Villa Medici with this demented swain dogging his steps. Bells rang out. A quarter of two. Ye gods. Dancey had not made directly for the Pincio because of the boy galloping at his side. He seemed to be spouting verse now, but it was difficult to tell. Everything in Italian rhymes with everything else.

Dancey stopped and the boy, misreading this as a hopeful sign, clutched Dancey's hand, the one that grasped the strap of the shoulder bag. To move his hand would have rendered the bag vulnerable, so Dancey found himself holding hands with a boy on the sidewalk, a boy whose breathing seemed dangerously apopleptic.

"*Signora,* let me buy you a coffee." They had stopped in front of a café.

Dancey hesitated, then said demurely. "I would prefer wine."

"Excellent. Come." His grip on Dancey's hand was painful as he pulled him toward a table.

"No, no, no. Not here. Not now. What is the number of your room?"

The boy's eyes bulged in triumph. "At the *pensione?*"

"Yes."

"Two-o-five! When will you come?"

Dancey pretended to think. "Soon. I will hurry."

"Yes. Hurry. You must come before my mother returns."

The assignation made, Dancey was free to go. He did not glance back, fearful that anything he did might be misunderstood by that frenetic faun of a boy. It was all he could do not to break into a run. He was going to be late. There was simply no way that he could arrive at the Villa Medici by two o'clock.

26

As a lesser angel would have observed them at the time, and as James Dancey reconstructed them later, these were the events of that fateful afternoon:

With Carter the deputy cultural attaché in tow, Polly entered the gardens of the Villa Medici and followed a hedge-lined path toward the imposing structure that housed the French Academy in Rome. The paths were peopled but not crowded; lovers sat upon the grass; nannies more sedately occupied stone benches; children cavorted. But Polly's eye was on the redheaded woman some twenty yards ahead of them on the path.

"What's the hurry?" Carter complained. He was working on his cone with a lateral lick and clearly did not enjoy being forced to combine hurried forward movement and the consumption of ice cream. Polly flung her own cone, a melting flame, into a bush.

"It's two o'clock."

"Then we're on time. Where's Dancey?"

Polly had the envelope of money under her arm, pressed close to her body, and she almost wished that it rendered her as vulnerable as Jim Dancey. They were closing the gap now and Polly could only marvel at the convincingness of Dancey's walk. Anyone would take him for a woman. She had to get the envelope to him.

Standing in the entrance of the building, Nathaniel Gainer spotted Polly, but he was damned if he could pick out any woman

as James Dancey. A red wig, Polly had told him. And then he saw
her. Him. Dancey. He must be the redheaded woman Polly was
following, indeed trying to catch. She had to get that envelope to
Dancey.

The redhead had been proceeding directly toward Gainer, but
suddenly he/she turned abruptly to the right and seemed to pick
up the pace. Gainer looked to where earlier he had located Ernesto
Cielli and his companion. This companion was Mario, Cielli's
driver, a man six feet in height, two hundred and thirty pounds,
very strong. Agile? Wait and see. In any case, the redhead was now
moving away from these two and Gainer, to his surprise, saw Cielli
pointing her out to Mario. The disguise must be known! Gainer
frowned. It would not do to have Dancey in danger from that
despicable Cielli. Polly had now caught up with the redhead and
was offering the envelope.

"I believe you dropped this, *signora*," Polly said, a lilt in her
voice. She banged at Dancey's arm with the envelope.

"I beg your pardon."

"Here. Take it . . ." Polly stopped. The woman was facing her
now and her expression was indignant. Polly leaned forward.
Dancey could not possibly be so transformed. "Jimmy?"

The woman drew herself up, inflating her massive breasts, and
sighted at Polly down a nose whose nostrils flared angrily. Her
eyes sparked and Polly feared that she was about to make a scene.

"Excuse me, *signora*. I have made a mistake."

Saying it was easier than believing it, she had been so certain
this was Dancey from the moment she had seen the red hair. Even
now, confronted by the incontrovertible fact that this was not
Jimmy, Polly nonetheless found the woman familiar. But of course
that was accountable for by the fact that her hair, or wig, was
identical to the *parrucca* Dancey had worn to her apartment.

"Where is Dancey?" the woman asked. The voice is the voice of
Jacob. . . . A woman had spoken, but it was Horne's voice Polly
heard. She stared at the redhead.

"Horne?"

"Mrs. Parson, if you don't mind." There was the lisp, and the

196

voice went up a register. "No one has reported seeing Dancey." A crackle in Mrs. Parson's bosom suggested a walkie-talkie and possible contact with unseen cohorts scattered about the gardens.

"I thought you were Dancey."

"Ho ho."

Cielli sat forward on his marble bench, his breath short and excited; the prospect of betraying everyone with whom he was involved affected him as other men are affected by the opportunity of heroism. The package containing the manuscript was on his knees, his eyes were on Polly Osborne and the redheaded woman. The business with the envelope suggested that the woman had to be Dancey. Cielli had not forgotten the guise in which Dancey had escaped from the Columbus Hotel. Cielli wet his lips. "Mario," he said softly. "Go get her."

Mario started toward Polly and the redhead, going in a straight line, ignoring the paths unless they coincided with the direct route to his destination. First the wig, Cielli had told him. First rip off the wig. It would not do to have people think that Mario was accosting an honest-to-God female in the park. Just let people see that it was Dancey prancing around in woman's clothes and there would be volunteers to help Mario hustle Dancey off to the car. Cielli smiled. He put the package beside him on the bench, convinced now that he could take Dancey without having to relinquish the manuscript. With Carlo Posti gone, he would once more have Zar's ear. He would urge upon him the merits of sensational kidnappings. A man like Nathaniel Gainer could be bled dry if they snatched his niece.

The sensation of being attacked from behind is difficult to describe, but even if Ernesto Cielli had been practiced in the verbalization of his experience, he would have been hard put to it to express in words what it was like when a strap dropped over his head and he was jerked backward, his rump a fulcrum. He looked up into the face of the redhead Mario had just gone for. Just before the rock hit his head, he heard whispered in his ear a word of explanation.

"This is for Giuseppe, you sonofabitch."

Polly, puzzled by the revelation that Mrs. Parson was Horne, not Dancey, stood staring at the undercover agent, whose own eyes looked past her and suddenly filled with apprehension. Horne dug in his bosom and pulled out a miniature walkie-talkie. Polly turned to see Mario bearing down upon them with relentless stride, his small eyes crinkled with determination. Perhaps the squint cut down his peripheral vision. In any case, he did not notice, as Polly did, Nathaniel Gainer approach from the direction of the villa, his cane at the ready. He thrust forward with precision, inserting the cane between Mario's ankles, and the huge man pitched forward with a quizzical expression on his face.

While this was going on, Polly heard Horne barking orders to his forces. She let out a cheer when Mario went down, and turned to see Horne's reaction to her uncle's deed. But Mrs. Parson in turn had turned and was scampering across the garden. Suddenly, from behind a massive plane tree, a young man stepped, his eyes afire with desire, an I-gotcha expression on his face, his arms widened in welcome. In a trice, he had enfolded Mrs. Parson in his embrace, stumbled with her to a nearby bench and moaning, sunk his lips upon her throat.

Polly was distracted from this startling if tender scene by the flash of Cielli's soles as he was toppled backward from his bench and coshed with a rock. The assailant, incredibly, was Mrs. Parson. But there was Mrs. Parson being fondled on a marble bench by a boiling broth of a boy. The second Mrs. Parson snatched a package from the bench on which Cielli had lately sat, hitched a large bag higher on her shoulder, and went loping away across the gardens in the direction of Trinità dei Monti.

Mario, struggling to his feet, looked wildly around. He could not see Cielli. A look of puzzlement and rage came over his face. It did not go away when he saw a redhead on a bench in the embrace of an apparent rapist. Mario grunted and plunged through a hedge toward this Rodinesque scene.

"Dancey!" he shouted.

Taking this as signal, half a dozen riflemen sprang up like mushrooms. They were clad entirely in black. They had nylon stockings pulled over their faces. As if in Mario's command, they closed in on the bench.

"Jimmy," Polly cried, starting off after the second Mrs. Parson. "Jimmy, wait for me."

27

Dancey, with the precious package under one arm and the bag of lire bouncing on his hip, could have shouted with triumph as he headed away from the Villa Medici. Arriving late had, in the event, been the deciding factor. Some commotion in the center of the garden had distracted Cielli and it had been a simple matter, with that huge companion drawn toward the commotion, to topple Cielli, whisper a remark of vindication, pick up the package and run.

His elation oozed away as he progressed. From various nooks and niches, from behind shrubs and statues, dozens of men emerged and fell in beside him as he ran. Their expressions were impassive and Dancey could not interpret them. He was surrounded as by a flying wedge. He slowed to a walk and his newly acquired consorts did the same. They seemed to be regarding him with respectful attention.

"Sir?" one of them said.

Sir? A downward glance told Dancey how he was dressed. He threw back his shoulders to maximize his bosom. A hand sent fluttering to his hair confirmed that the wig was in place. Good God! Had he overestimated the effectiveness of his disguise? What a moment to be hauled in on a morals charge. American transvestite pinched in Pincio. He looked about in panic and there, a mere stone's throw away, stood Carter finishing off an ice cream cone with concentrated devotion. Dancey pushed through his unwanted companions and confronted the junior diplomat.

"Carter, you have to help me."

Carter's mouth was full of ice cream and his eyes were full of wonder. He tried unsuccessfully to speak.

"Tell these men who I am."

Carter swallowed. "With pleasure. Who are you?" A stern look appeared on his face. "Who are they?"

"I don't know."

"Who are you men?" Carter demanded, his voice trembling. He was becoming fully conscious of the number and size of the stolid men surrounding this female. Immediately, with choral precision, a dozen hands produced a dozen leather wallets and flipped them open in Carter's face. Dancey, confirmed in his worst fears, resumed his flight. By God, they would not take him without a struggle.

He vaulted a hedge and fairly flew down the road. The sound of his thumping heart was accompanied by the authoritative footfalls of his pursuers, who, unaccountably, seemed deliberately to keep a pace or two behind him. From farther back came the crackle of gunfire.

At the Spanish Steps, Dancey started down, leaping over seated hippies, careening around flower stalls, bowling angry ascenders from his path. So heedless was his descent that he was sure he was shaking off his pursuers. And so he was. A glance over his shoulder revealed that they were high above him, unable to force their way through the crowd on the steps. Unfortunately, that confirming glance caused Dancey to miss his step. A sandal slid out from under him and, completely out of control, he windmilled into a flower stall.

It was instinct that made him put out a hand to break his fall. It was choice that dictated that it was not the hand that gripped the invaluable Thomistic autograph. Released, his shoulder bag flew centrifugally away and spun high in the air, where its flap opened and lire by the thousands rained on the Piazza di Spagna. Confronted by a miracle not unlike that summer day's when snow fell on the church of St. Mary Major, Romans, tourists and hippies fell upon the money that fell upon themselves. Dancey, struggling to

202

his feet, brushing gardenias from his bosom, saw his money disappearing like snowflakes before the summer sun. He would have liked to enter the fray and rescue some fraction of his ill-gotten gains, but his pursuers, though further slowed by the howling, scrambling mob chasing ten-thousand-lire notes, were still intent on reaching him. Buridan's ass, in the medieval fable, placed equidistant between two piles of hay, starved of indecision. Dancey regarded escape as more important than his dwindling fortune. He turned right into the piazza, zipped past the Babington English Tea Room and, his destination now clear to him, homed in on the underground toilets which were overlooked by Babington's.

Down the steps and into the Ladies, alone at last, past the attendant who dwelt in those depths as in some unsavory Dantesque circle, he plunged into a booth and pulled the door shut behind him.

"Jimmy! Jimmy, where are you?"

Huddled in the stall, trying to catch his breath, hugging his package and trying not to think of all those lovely lire scudding across the cobbles of the Piazza di Spagna and being scooped up by greedy hands, Dancey could not believe his ears.

"Polly?"

"Yes!"

There was a tap on the door of the stall. Dancey opened it. Polly had never looked better to him, never more desirable. She carried an envelope and his shoulder bag, considerably depleted. Her expression flickered from relief to amusement to tenderness. Dancey stepped out of the stall and took her in his arms. The attendant, seated at her table, looked up, considered the embracing couple for a moment, shrugged, then resumed the counting of her coins.

Five minutes later, a young man and woman emerged from the underground women's rest room in the Piazza di Spagna. She dangled a red wig. He clutched two packages to the breast of his wrinkled shirt. They were holding hands. One would have said they were lovers. A platoon of puzzled men stood in disarray in the square. The couple approached one of the men and the young lady handed over the red wig.

"Give this to Horne."

The man produced a walkie-talkie and made bewildered inquiries of the ether. Suddenly the squawky voice of his chief, whom he and his fellows had followed down the Spanish Steps and seen disappear in his customary drag into the women's rest room, addressed them electronically from the Pincio above, ordering them to get the hell up there as quickly as possible. The rest of the communication was garbled, but it sounded as if Horne had said he was being raped.

The young couple, radiant, bumping hips, crossed the piazza and, pausing so that he could stoop to pluck a single ten-thousand-lire note from the gutter, turned into the Via Condotti and disappeared.

28

The Villa Strommer, half in shadow, half in sunlight, offered on this lovely September day the best of both worlds, indeed the best of several worlds, or so it seemed to Dr. James Dancey, the first curator of the Gainer Library housed in the villa, as well as the first director of the Research Academy underwritten by funds from the Gainer Foundation. Light and shadow played upon his closed lids, the autumn air quickened his quintessentially academic soul, reminding him of the annual return to classroom and study. As it had for so many years, September brought with it the promise of new beginnings and the renewal of the familiar routine of scholarship. And now he had the sinecure every scholar dreams of.

"What are you thinking about?" Polly asked.

His head was in her lap. From time to time, she dropped a grape into his mouth. Shakespeare, thou shouldst be living at this hour. "Country matters," he said.

"Well, this is the place for it."

"Indeed."

She smiled down at him. He smiled up at her. They would regularize their union after Polly's annulment came through. It seemed that Osborne, her first husband, had vowed never to have children and the Church sensibly took this to be in contradiction to the marriage vow. Polly herself thought that not having children was one of the nicest things Osborne could do for mankind, but she had been persuaded not to voice this biased though perhaps accurate assessment. Polly had far more sympathy for the victims of the summer just past than for her former husband.

The remnant of Ottobre Quindici that showed up at the Villa Medici had had scarcely more chance of survival than they had given poor Porres. While Horne was being ravished and his men were pursuing Dancey down the Spanish Steps, three Israeli commandos and a contingent of Swiss Guards had rounded up Ottobre Quindici. All but one had dropped their weapons without demur. The exception, Zar, firing wildly as he went, made a break toward the Pincio. He died where he fell. Meanwhile, Italian plainclothesmen took Cielli and Mario into custody. A disheveled Horne, vowing that he would bring charges against the youth who had undone him, was hurried away by his men. Minutes later, so Nathaniel Gainer claimed, the lovers and nannies and children were back in place.

"Poor Strommer," Dancey said.

"Yes."

It was difficult not to think of Ulrich Strommer, living in a villa named for him. Strommer's death was the one that still made Dancey shiver. Giuseppe's less so. The little porter had been a supernumerary in life and Dancey found it difficult to adopt a God's-eye view of Giuseppe's importance. Porres had been avenged. As for Carlo Posti, the phony Nerone, Strommer's murderer, his death could seem the execution of poetic justice. A fall goes before a fall.

The surviving members of Ottobre Quindici denied everything. They claimed to have been hired by Zar under the pretext of shooting a movie scene at the Villa Medici. Zar was not there to confirm or deny their story. They had not known their guns were loaded. Would they be found guilty? The justice of men is an imperfect thing. Thus Dancey need not worry about the money he had scattered about the Piazza di Spagna, at least from the point of view of prosecution. The money had been Cielli's. Zar had ordered him to add fifty thousand dollars of his own money to Dancey's account, in order to further the deception. It was an account Ottobre Quindici had thought they could tap. At least Posti had tried to. Cielli now languished in a Neapolitan prison. It seemed an inadequate end for the man Horne had called a virtuoso of treachery.

206

"Cielli is a sonofabitch," Nathaniel Gainer said, and that was inadequate too.

The old man was a frequent visitor to the Villa Strommer, but his motive was not that of a benefactor intent on surveying the effects of his generosity. He spent most of his time in the villa library with Père Jacques, who, restored to consciousness, pursued a full recovery in this hilly seclusion before returning to the Vatican Library. The little Franciscan was only sporadically curious about the events he had missed during his stay at Salvator Mundi. He was content that the purloined manuscript was back where it belonged. Every morning at seven he offered Mass at an improvised altar in the villa library and Dancey was pleased to hear a daily commemoration for Ulrich Strommer. The loyalty of medievalists was unlikely to stop at the grave.

Dancey himself, as if by way of retribution, devoted an hour each day to a reading of those parts of Aquinas's *Summa contra gentiles* contained in the manuscript he had been instrumental in removing from the Vatican Library. The text he read was the printed one of the Leonine edition, the huge volume propped up before him on his desk. An hour before, Polly had come upon him while he was perusing the thirtieth chapter of the third book.

"Read it to me," she said.

"It's in Latin."

"So translate."

Dancey paraphrased. "Man's highest good is not a matter of luck, since luck occurs apart from any use of the mind and man's proper goal must be pursued and achieved knowingly. But luck reigns supreme in the acquisition of wealth. Therefore, human happiness cannot consist in riches."

"Hmmm."

"He has other arguments to the same effect."

"That one will do."

"You're easily satisfied. Philosophically."

"Oh, I don't know. Think of you and that bag full of money."

He groaned. "I'd rather not."

Might it not have been considered an instance of what Aquinas called occult compensation if Dancey had retained Cielli's money?

Carter had made a fuss over the government's five thousand, but that had been a short-lived annoyance. From the Georgetown alumni magazine, Dancey had learned that Carter was now stationed in Istanbul. There was a photo of him, wearing a fez.

Polly and Dancey had come out onto this open porch that overlooked a valley twisting away in the direction of Rome. And there, regardless of preference, Dancey thought of the money that had filled the air in the Piazza di Spagna several months before. It had come to its new owners without rhyme or reason. To benefit from a cloudburst of lire would scarcely have been a rational reason for going to the piazza. No more could his possession of the money be attributed to the fulfillment of any plan of his. Luck. What befalls us, good or bad, does not make us what we morally are. No doubt Aquinas was right, though Dancey did not see how his new position, Polly, or the security of the Villa Strommer were any less matters of luck. Yet it would have been difficult to deny that he was happy. Perhaps further reading of St. Thomas would clarify the matter.

Polly's fingers traveled through his hair, parting it, searching. She might have been a mother monkey looking for lice. He told her this.

"It has to be somewhere."

"Forget the microdot, Polly."

"Micronesia?"

"Ho ho."

Of course he did not want her to forget it. He did not want her to find it either. Happiness lies in the search. Not Aquinas. Lessing? It did not matter. Of course it was not Horne's imaginary microdot, but the transmitter she sought. It had stopped sending. Horne had advised against having recourse to the scanner that could have located it.

"The damned thing scrambles your hormones."

A guarded explanation of Horne's fey manner and penchant for women's clothing? Do not microfiche in troubled waters. Horne had been transferred to Oslo.

Dancey preferred to think of the transmitter as a microdot embedded under his skin, containing a record of terrorist mis-

208

deeds. This enabled him to think of it as Original Sin, his burden, a common guilt, a reminder that we are all in need of mercy. What man does not carry about with him a personal record of wrongdoing, however invisible to the naked eye? The transmitter become a microdot had become a metaphor.

"And what awful things have you done?" Polly wanted to know.

The truth was that, at the moment, he felt an almost prelapsarian innocence. In similar circumstances, he understood, confessing Catholics mentioned some sins of their past lives.

"Well, I voted for Nixon."

Polly thought about that for a moment, then said, "So did Nixon."

A nearby cypress swayed in the wind. Crows cawed. Polly fed Dancey another grape. Spinning on its axis, the earth moved around the sun. Happiness is no accident. In a little while they would go inside and have a drink.